SNAPPER

Also by
PETER MALONEY
AND FELICIA ZEKAUSKAS

CHILDREN'S PICTURE BOOKS

The Magic Hockey Stick
One Foot, Two Feet
Redbird at Rockefeller Center
Belly Button Boy
His Mother's Nose
Bronto Eats Meat
Just Schoolin' Around Series

SNAPPER

PETER MALONEY
AND FELICIA ZEKAUSKAS

DON'T EVEN THINK ABOUT GOING INTO THE LAKE

Redbird House

Hackensack

ISBN-13: 978-0-9859321-1-4
ISBN-10: 0985932112

For Christian and Ian

With thanks to Fran Bouchoux, Cheryl Best, Carolyn Kegel, Manette Begin-Loudon, Jane Matich, Derek Reist and extra special thanks to our friend and neighbor, David Lender, for his help and patience in shepherding this work into the real world.

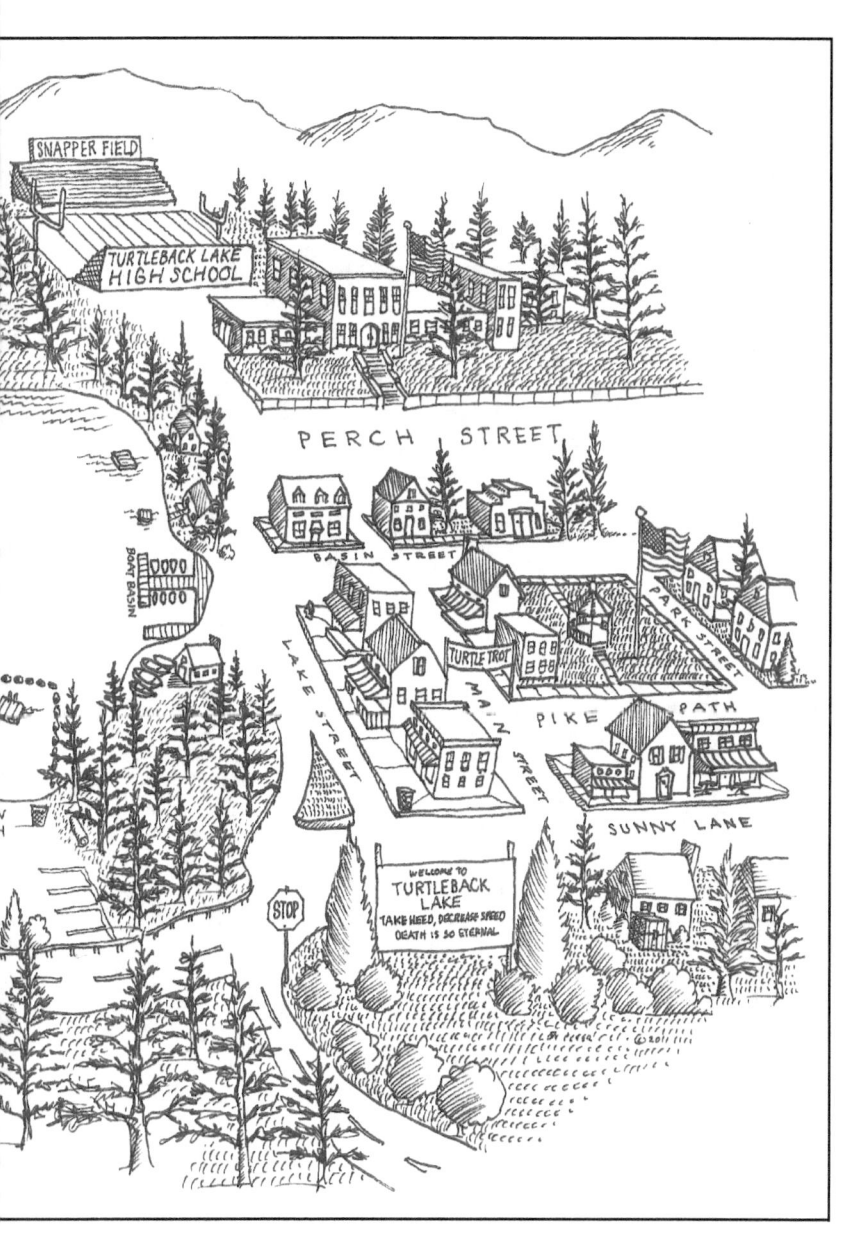

Chapter 1

Turtleback Lake 1967

Bill Sat On The Deck and gazed out at the lake, eyeing the docks that bobbed forty to fifty yards offshore. Every summer for as long as he could remember, Bill and his best friend, Oscar, had been swimming out to them.

But another summer diving off the same old docks just wasn't going to do it. This summer, Bill needed something new, something to test his mettle.

And there it was – right where it had always been – smack dab in the middle of the lake: the long low white rock that gave both the lake and the town their names.

Turtleback Rock.

For years, Turtleback Rock had seemed as remote and unattainable as the moon. But using a pair of binoculars he'd gotten for his birthday, Bill had been bringing the rock closer and closer – so close that he could practically look into the eyes of the snapping turtles that lazed in the hot sun on the rock's bleached white surface.

There had always been something vaguely sinister about the rock. Rumors said that the rock was surrounded by a ring of whirlpools that would suck down anyone who dared to come close to it.

"What a load of crap!" Bill said to Oscar. "There's nothing around that rock but water."

Bill had just told Oscar his big plan. It had been on his mind for days.

"Forget it," said Oscar. "I can't swim that far. That rock's gotta be a mile from shore. And what if what they say about the whirlpools is true?"

Bill expected this. Oscar was his closest friend, but he was definitely on the cautious side when it came to water. Out on the football field it was another story. There, Oscar was a totally different person: lightning fast and fearless. He was the star of the Snappers – the Turtleback Lake High School football team.

But summer vacation had just begun. Football practice was an eternity away. And Bill needed someone – namely Oscar – to share in his heroics.

"We're not gonna swim to it," said Bill. "We're going to take a canoe."

"And what if it tips over?" said Oscar. "We'll be a mile from shore."

"So wear a lifejacket," said Bill.

Oscar was desperate for any excuse not to go.

"My parents will kill me," he said. "And there's no way my mother wouldn't see us. She's at the kitchen window all day long."

Oscar hated disappointing Bill. Best friends weren't that easy to come by. But the truth was, Bill's idea of fun wasn't always his. It was just hard to come right out and say it.

"Don't worry about your mamma," said Bill. "She won't see us."

"Yeah? Why not?"

"Because we're going at night."

Night! Night was a thousand times worse than day. The lake at night gave Oscar the creeps. People said Turtleback Lake was as deep as the mountains around it. At night, things came up from the bottom. The last thing Oscar wanted to do was to go out on the lake in the dark. But he couldn't tell Bill. He knew exactly what Bill would do. He'd flap his elbows against his side and strut about squawking, "*Bawk, bawk, bawk, bawk, bawk! Chicken!*"

* * *

It was past nine when Bill met Oscar down at the edge of the lake. Both boys had climbed out of their bedroom windows and then lowered themselves to the ground.

Now Oscar was sitting on the canoe's forward thwart and Bill was standing knee-deep in the water a few feet from shore. Bill gave the canoe a strong shove, hopped in the back, and took a seat in the stern.

Oscar turned around to face him.

"Hey – it's pitch black out here," he said. "How are we even gonna find the rock?"

"Just wait," said Bill.

And then, as if on cue, the moon began rising over the mountains that rimmed the lake's eastern shore. Within minutes, the moon was high and bright and full enough to make the rock in the middle of the lake glow a ghostly white.

Dragging his paddle in the water, Bill steered the canoe from the stern, while up near the bow Oscar plunged and pulled like a slave on a Roman galley. But when Oscar looked down at his feet, there were no chains around his ankles, nor was there any whip lashing his back. No one was forcing him to be here. If anything, he was here because of his own damned weakness. He could hear his mother's voice chastising him: "So, if Bill Lupo jumps off the Brooklyn Bridge, you're going to jump, too?"

But what did it matter now? The only way out was to dive into the cold black water and swim back to shore. It was too late for that. Oscar was now along for the ride. There was no getting out and no turning back.

Chapter 2

Turtleback Lake 1927

"YOU *WHAT?*" said Wilhelmina Andersen, glaring at her husband across the kitchen table.

"I bought the property," said Owen.

Wilhelmina could've killed him on the spot. They had discussed the matter over and over, and every time, Wilhelmina had said the same thing: "No!"

The money they had saved was for the future.

Still, for weeks Owen had carried around a half-inch advertisement that he had cut out of the newspaper. *"Piece of Paradise,"* said the ad, *"wooded lakefront acre perfect for cabin, cottage, summer home."* Every day during his breaks at the bottling plant, Owen sneaked a peak at the little softened piece of newsprint he kept in his pocket. Then one day, despite his wife's repeated objections, the pull got too strong.

"So now what?" fumed Wilhelmina. "Now what are we going

to do?"

"We're going to build on it," said Owen.

"With what?" asked Wilhelmina. "We haven't got a penny left."

"I don't need money to build," said Owen. "I've got tools. I've got two good hands. And I've got Isaac."

Isaac was their son, their only child.

"So now you think about Isaac?" she scoffed. "You should have thought about him before you bought this, this, this piece of paradise!"

Wilhelmina spat out the words – piece of paradise – as if they were bits of grit that had gotten into her mouth.

"That money could've gone toward college!"

"And Isaac needs college for what?" asked Owen. "Did I go to college? Did you? Working with me, Isaac will learn something he can actually use. Like how to build something!"

For the next year, Isaac's weekends were lost to him. Every Friday afternoon, as his classmates burst out of school, Isaac would trudge toward a black Model A Ford where his father sat in the driver's seat waiting for him.

"Ready, Isaac?" he'd ask as Isaac plopped into the front seat.

"Dad, do we really have to?" Isaac pleaded.

"Yes, Isaac, we do," answered his father. "And someday you'll be glad we did. Someday you'll have something no one can ever take away from you."

* * *

"This is how America was made," said Owen.

He and Isaac were sitting in the flickering light of a campfire, eating baked beans straight from the can.

"We're like the early settlers who went west into lands unknown and used whatever they found to build shelter for themselves," waxed Owen. "We're following in our forefathers' footsteps."

"But Nana and Papa settled in Brooklyn," said Isaac. "They never moved west of the East River."

Owen sighed.

Why was it that his son always got bogged down in literal details when it was the big picture he was trying to give him?

"That's not the point, Isaac," explained Owen. "The point is they had the courage to start new lives in a new land. It's the imperative to move forward that brought them here to these shores."

Owen made a sweeping gesture – as if the "shores" they had come to were the shores of Turtleback Lake itself.

"What does 'imperative' mean?" asked Isaac.

Owen peered through the trunks of the dark trees. The lake beyond was plated in silvery moonlight. Out in the middle, Owen could see the small white rock island whose domed surface always made him think of a human skull. It was glowing now in the moonlight.

"An imperative is something you must do," explained Owen. "It's something that has more control over you than you have over it."

"I think I have an imperative, Dad."

Isaac rose from the tree stump he'd been sitting on.

"I'll be back in a minute," he said.

Isaac made his way through the trees down to the lake. Recently, he had made up a game to amuse himself. He was trying to write his name in pee. His goal was to pee his whole name – Isaac Christian Andersen. But now, even in the light of the moon, it was too dark for that. So Isaac made up a new game. He'd see how many rocks he could pee on before his urine ran out. He started with the furthest rock he could reach and worked his way inward.

Isaac had just splashed his twelfth stone and was squirting the thirteenth when it happened. The rock moved.

At first, Isaac just blinked. It had to be an illusion, a trick of the moonlight and the gentle breeze that was rippling the water. But blinking changed nothing. The rock was definitely moving. It was coming closer and getting bigger. Now it was just a few feet from shore and it had grown to the size of an overturned wheelbarrow.

Isaac's eyes widened in amazement, and then in horror: a large reptilian head suddenly reared up. Two sunburst yellow eyes fixed on Isaac.

The creature opened its hooked, beaked mouth and let out a long, low hiss. Isaac stood frozen. Then the creature lunged. Isaac spun around and started crashing back through the woods to the clearing where his father was bent over a basin of sudsy dishwater, washing spoons.

Chapter 3

Turtleback Lake September 2006

JUDD CLAYTON STOOD before the school board.

"Look," he said. "Let's not mince words. My concern here tonight is property values. Any and all negative perceptions of our town must be addressed and eliminated. And I believe the name of our football team has become a problem."

Judd's position was hardly devoid of self-interest. As the owner of Clayton Realty, *"Turtleback Lake's Leading Home Seller For Over A Quarter Century,"* Judd wanted every home to sell for top dollar.

Still, the members of the board looked stunned by the audacity of Judd's suggestion.

Silence lingered until Dr. Deena Goode, the town's high school principal, spoke.

"Really, Mr. Clayton," she began, affecting her most reasonable tone. "You're not seriously suggesting that the name of the high school football team is adversely effecting property values?"

Judd Clayton stared into Deena's brown eyes.

Dr. Goode had been principal for less than a month. She wouldn't even be the principal if it weren't for Judd. Yet, now, here the two of them were – at odds.

"Without a doubt there's an effect," said Judd.

"Perhaps then," said Deena, "perhaps you could provide us with some *unbiased* statistical data to support your thesis?"

Judd was livid. This was just the kind of supercilious, pseudo-academic mumbo jumbo that Dr. Goode – Deena – used to make her every utterance seem indisputably correct.

"Well, Doctor," began Judd, barely able to conceal his anger. "I forgot to bring along my graphs and bar charts, but I can tell you this: That recent article in *The Turtleback Gazette* has been mentioned by three of the last four people I've shown homes to."

The article in the local paper was about the increased number of bathers who had been bitten – 'attacked' was the reporter's unfortunate choice of words – by snapping turtles that summer. None had been serious, nothing more than little nips really, but still – it was statistically irrefutable – there definitely had been an increase over previous summers. Then again, snapping turtles were in every lake in the mountains of North Jersey. It was a lot better than having water moccasins.

"So let me clarify your position," said Dr. Goode. "You're saying that the name "Snappers" might cause prospective homebuyers to think twice about buying in Turtleback Lake?"

"That's exactly what I'm saying," said Judd.

Dr. Goode shook her head. She was not the only one ready to dismiss Judd's proposal without further discussion.

Head coach Bill Lupo was silently seething in his seat. Bill had been the center – the snapper – for the high school football team back in the sixties. In Bill's opinion, the Snapper name was an institution. It was something carved in stone, an inseparable part of the town's identity.

Though she wasn't ready to admit it here and now, Dr. Goode wasn't particularly fond of the team's moniker. "The Snappers" struck her as hostile and aggressive. But an odd dynamic had sprung up between Judd and her. She felt an almost irresistible compulsion to disagree with him.

"And let me remind everyone of one more thing," said Judd. "The more homes sell for, the higher they'll be appraised. And the higher they're appraised, the higher they'll be taxed."

Judd paused and looked around at the members of the board.

"And where do you think the money for our teachers' salaries comes from?" he said. "And what do you think pays for our athletic programs?"

Judd paused again to let the logic of his argument sink in.

"Property taxes," he said, "are the life blood of this town."

Dr. Goode gave Judd a look she had perfected during her years as a vice-principal. The look had withered even the biggest, most recalcitrant troublemakers. But Judd didn't wither – he simply glared back.

"Mr. Clayton," she said finally, tiring of the showdown. "I can assure you that all of us here appreciate your concern for the security of our positions. So it will no doubt please you to know that the rejection of your proposal is in no way influenced by a desire for professional gain or financial advancement. The name of our football team will remain what it has always been – The Snappers."

"Here, here," muttered Bill Lupo. "Now let's get the hell out of here."

Judd's son – Judd Junior – was walking into the locker room when Coach Lupo called him into his office.

"Get in here, JJ," he said. "And take a seat."

"What is it, coach?" said JJ. Coach Lupo had never before called him into his office.

"That was some performance your daddy put on last night," said Coach Lupo.

JJ looked puzzled.

"Don't just sit there looking dumbfounded!" said Coach Lupo.

"But I don't know what you're talking about, sir."

"Well," said Coach Lupo. "Maybe you and your daddy can have a little heart to heart and he can fill you in."

Then Coach Lupo turned to his assistant, George Jenkins.

"What do you think, Georgie?" he said. "You got any names you think might improve local property values for JJ's dad?"

"Gee, Bill, I don't know," said George. "How about the Tadpoles? Or the Pollywogs? Or wait – hold on – how about the Lily Pads?"

"What do you think, JJ?" said Coach Lupo. "Think your daddy would like it if we changed the team's name to the Turtleback Lake Lily Pads?"

JJ didn't know where to look, let alone what to say. He stared down at his hands.

"Get out of here," said Coach Lupo. "And put on your pads – your lily pads!"

"We'll have full contact today," Bill said to George as soon as JJ left. "It's time these kids learned why you need a hard shell in life."

The confrontation with Coach Lupo was just the beginning. When JJ got to his locker, most of the varsity football team was waiting for him.

"I need something," said Bobby Savarese. "Something in your locker."

Bobby Savarese was the fiercest player ever to roam Snapper Field. To freshmen, he was a legend – and a terror.

"Open it," he said.

JJ dialed his combination in plain sight of everyone. There didn't seem any point in trying to hide it. Then he swung open his locker's vented metal door. His jersey, pants, and jock strap were hanging from hooks up top. His cleats, socks, and pads were jumbled in a pile at the bottom.

Savarese elbowed JJ aside and thrust his arm into the locker. When he withdrew his hand, he was clutching JJ's jock strap.

"Do you know what happens to softies?" said Savarese, bringing the tip of his flattened nose to within an inch of JJ's.

JJ didn't answer.

"I said, 'Do you know what happens to softies?'"

"No," stammered JJ. He could barely get the word out.

"Give me the hammer!" spat Savarese.

A large rubber mallet was passed through the crowd till it reached Savarese. He gripped its long wooden handle in his right hand.

He placed the jock on the wooden bench in front of JJ's locker.

"Softies," he said, his voice now barely a whisper. "Get smashed!"

Savarese brought the head of the hammer down onto JJ's jock. The hard plastic cup, encased in a snapped pouch, split in half.

"They get smashed," he said, "into tiny little pieces."

Savarese raised the hammer back up above his head and

brought it down again, and again, and again. When he finally stopped pounding, he glared at JJ with eyes that bulged from their sockets.

JJ stood silent, stunned.

Savarese looked down at JJ's feet and spat on the ground. A gob of spit clung to the toe of JJ's sneaker.

"Show's over," he said, turning to the players gathered behind him. "Let's get on with practice."

As the locker room emptied, JJ sat down on the bench in front of his locker and unsnapped his jock strap. He dumped the shattered bits into the trash bin. Today he'd have to practice without proper protection.

JJ tried to suit up as fast as he could, but his trembling fingers wouldn't cooperate. It took forever to strap on his shoulder pads, pull on his jersey, and tie the laces of his cleats.

Then he squeezed his head into his helmet and snapped the chinstrap. JJ looked fully padded, but he knew how vulnerable he really was.

* * *

JJ finally emerged from the locker room and stepped into the bright September sun. The rest of the team was already running drills out on the practice field.

JJ ran down the locker room steps, his metal cleats clattering on the concrete stairs. He broke into a run that took him directly past a cluster of cheerleaders gathered beneath a goal post.

The cheerleaders were all good-looking – it seemed to be a prerequisite of the job – but one was absolutely, unbelievably beautiful.

Mary Robinson.

JJ had never seen anyone who even compared. When he saw her for the first time on the first day of school, it was love at first sight. She was almost too beautiful to look at.

But now, sprinting past the cheerleaders, JJ risked a glance in her direction.

JJ was jolted. It was like being hit by lightning. Mary Robinson was looking right back at him! The gaze of her beautiful blue eyes came straight through the bars of his facemask and met his.

JJ fell to the ground like he'd been shot.

"Oh, God!" he muttered. "What a clod!"

His cleats had snagged on the turf. When he hit the ground, his helmet twisted to the side. A tuft of grass poked through the ear hole.

Looking out from within the shell of his helmet, JJ had a turtle's eye view of a dozen pairs of black and white saddle shoes. One pair broke away from the pack. They came pattering toward him then stopped less than a foot from his face.

Starting at the shoes, JJ's eyes began to climb: Up past the short white ankle socks, up the tanned, slender calves, up over the knees and thighs to the pleated black skirt, up over the white knit sweater with the bright yellow-and-black snapping turtle emblem, up to the rounded white collar opened at the throat.

JJ's heart was beating too fast to go any higher.

Mary knelt down.

"Are you okay?" she asked.

"I'm fine," said JJ.

Mary smiled at him. Then she leaned in a little closer and in a voice that only JJ could hear, she started to cheer: *"Hey, Ho, 24! Pick yourself up off the floor!"*

JJ smiled and rose to his knees. Then he straightened his helmet and brushed the dirt off his pants.

"Thanks," he said, "for…"

JJ paused and looked into Mary's beautiful blue eyes.

"For cheering me up."

"Anytime," said Mary.

Marc Bozian felt lucky.

He was on the right track. Last year, less than a month out of college, Marc had landed a job as a reporter for *The Turtleback Gazette*.

"I know it's not *The Times* or *The Record*," he had told his parents. "But it's a start – a stepping stone to bigger and better things."

Marc got an apartment above a storefront in downtown Turtleback Lake. He spent the next year covering grand openings, town council meetings, and local sporting events. But then, out of the blue, the gods gave Marc what he'd been secretly praying for: a story with real teeth.

It was a warm Saturday in early September. Marc had the day off, but as he constantly reminded himself, a real reporter is never truly off. He was at the town beach reading an Edwin Corley novel when a sudden shriek made him look up from the page.

The lifeguard on duty, Cliff Marine, leaped from his stand and dashed across the sand. In just seconds he was in the lake, swimming out to a little girl who was thrashing in the water near the floating dock.

The girl screamed again.

"Help!" she cried. "Something bit me!"

Cliff had seen this moment in his mind a million times. It was the moment he had trained for and dreamed about for years. He could practically see the newspaper clippings pressed flat in his mother's scrapbook.

Cliff quickly swam around the girl. Her arms and legs were flailing wildly. Cliff was cautious. The last thing he needed now was an elbow in the eye or a heel to the groin. Drowning people were dangerous, and though Cliff had practiced this maneuver dozens of times, it had always been with someone who wasn't actually drowning.

He swung his arm across the girl's chest and pinned down her arms.

"It's okay," he told her. "You're going to be okay."

For the first time, Cliff saw who it was. It was Joanne Sully. She was eight, maybe nine. Cliff knew her father. Jack Sully was a local painter who got jobs more for his reasonable rates than the quality of his work. Since his wife had left him, Jack had taken to drinking. Cliff knew all this because his parents had hired Jack the winter before to paint their den. Mr. Sully had draped the whole room with drop cloths then hadn't come back for weeks. Then he painted the room the wrong color.

"Something bit me," Joanne whimpered. "Hard."

"Just stay calm," Cliff told the little girl as he towed her back toward shore. Cliff was hoping that somebody was getting pictures of all this. Then he looked back at the water behind them. He almost gagged. The water had turned red with billowing clouds of blood.

"Hang in there," he said to the girl. "It's going to be okay."

But he was no longer even sure that this was true.

* * *

As Cliff was racing to the water, several people were already pressing 911 on their cell phone keypads. By the time he was wading back toward shore with the girl in his arms, an ambulance from the Turtleback Lake Rescue Squad was pulling up onto the scene.

The photographs Cliff had always imagined – the hero shots of him, the buff young lifeguard, emerging from the water with a girl draped in his arms – were captured on several digital cameras. They reproduced beautifully in *The Turtleback Gazette*.

The paramedics dashed across the beach and met Cliff waist deep in the water. They took the girl from his arms and carried her back to a collapsible gurney that was waiting at water's edge.

Paul Murphy took one look at the girl's foot.

"Jesus!" he muttered.

The blood was pouring out, fast and furious.

Down at the station, Paul was affectionately known as "the great coagulator." Nobody staunched blood better than Paul. But Paul had his work cut out for him. Joanne's foot was a gusher. He immediately elevated the injured limb and wrapped it quickly in gauze. Within seconds, the dressing was soaked through. As Paul removed the first blood-soaked wad, Marc Bozian peeked in for a closer look.

"Good God!" he gasped.

Where Joanne Sully's big toe should've been, there was nothing. The toe was completely gone, clipped clean to the bone. A bandage wasn't going to be enough. Paul quickly applied a tourniquet around the little girl's calf.

As the medics rolled the gurney back to the ambulance, Marc scanned the beach. Cliff Marine was alone, sitting on a log at the edge of a grassy clearing. Marc walked toward him, pulling out his pen and pad.

"Hey, Cliff!" called Marc. "I was hoping to get a few quick

words from you."

Cliff had always imagined being interviewed after a heroic rescue. He knew exactly the kinds of things he was going to say. They were like lines in a play he knew by heart. Only the lines weren't coming now. When Cliff opened his mouth, a torrent of vomit burst out.

Marc stopped and turned. He'd get Cliff's comments later.

* * *

When Marc Bozian's story appeared on the front page of a special Sunday edition of *The Turtleback Gazette,* the whole town pretty much already knew everything. The story had spread like wildfire. And as it spread, the details got gorier and gorier.

Soon it wasn't just Joanne's toe that was missing – it was her whole foot, her whole leg; in some accounts, she had lost her entire lower body.

That's what made Marc's account so important. It was his job to set the record straight. He had to provide facts where rumors and hearsay had taken hold. But Marc was determined to do even more. Marc intended to get to the bottom of the disturbing increase in the number of snapper attacks at Turtleback Lake. It was something that could no longer be ignored.

Every year, the pep rally before The Snappers' season opener against Elkskin Lake got bigger and wilder. This year, a towering teepee of wood had been erected in the parking lot behind the stadium scoreboard. Now it was a flaming inferno that sent sparks shooting high up into the starry night sky.

A throbbing mass of players, students and cheerleaders danced and whirled around the blazing fire. The skin on the cheerleaders' legs flashed red and gold as they shook and shimmied. Suddenly a pompom held too close to the fire burst into a ball of flames and was tossed into the inferno. Then one of the players grabbed a megaphone and began to chant.

"Skin the Elks! Skin the Elks! Skin the Elks!"

Soon the whole crowd was chanting along.

JJ stood at the back of the crowd, his hands thrust into his pockets. As he looked over the sea of bobbing heads, several cheerleaders were hoisted into the air.

The crowd started chanting, *"Snappers! Snappers! Snappers!"*

For the first time, JJ saw Mary. Someone was holding her high above his head, with his grubby fingers gripping the bare flesh of her inner thighs. Whoever was holding her began to spin her slowly round. With her legs spread wide, JJ could see the shiny golden panties Mary was wearing beneath her pleated skirt. The metallic fabric glinted in the firelight.

JJ rose up on his toes to see who was holding her. He could only make out the number on the back of his jersey. It was number 42: Bobby Savarese.

The chanting grew louder and faster. *"Snappers!"* now sounded like *"Snap her! Snap her! Snap her!"*

As JJ watched, Savarese extended his arms in a wide vee above his head. Mary's legs spread out in a full split. Then, leering at the crowd, Savarese tilted back his head and flicked his pointed pink tongue in and out like a snake.

Mary gazed out at the throng. Her eyes were shining. She had no idea what was going on beneath her pleated black skirt. She just beamed and waved, like a beauty queen on a float in a parade. In the radiating heat of the fire, JJ's blood rose to a boil.

Judd Clayton was taking Dan and Rebecca Woods on a tour of downtown Turtleback Lake. It was something he did whenever he felt his clients were getting serious.

"It looks like a Norman Rockwell painting," said Rebecca, eyeing the quaint storefronts lining Lake Street.

"Like the cover of *The Saturday Evening Post*," said Judd.

Rebecca Woods smiled.

"It's like we've stepped back in time," she said. "It could be 1965."

Judd smiled. The Woods were selling themselves.

In a world that was changing at an alarming rate, the idea of living in a community that stayed the same was very appealing – especially to couples with young children.

This was the Woods' second visit to Turtleback Lake. They'd driven all the way from Manhattan twice now. They *had* to be serious. They'd even left their two kids behind this time. Maybe they were ready to talk turkey.

With just the slightest thrust of his chin, Judd directed the Woods' gaze toward Drucker's General Store.

On Drucker's front porch was a large mechanical turtle. It was painted a bright yellow – just like the high school team's Snapper emblem. A child – Judd thought it might be Bill Lupo's granddaughter – climbed onto the turtle's back. She slipped her feet into the stirrups and dropped a coin into the slot. The turtle began rocking back and forth, its webbed claws moving in a circular swimming motion as its beaked mouth opened and closed.

"Oh, the kids would just *love* riding on that!" Dan said to Rebecca.

"I used to ride on it myself," said Judd. "Only back then, it was just a nickel. I think it might be a dime now, maybe it's even up to a quarter."

Judd wanted the Woods to know that he was more than just a broker. He was also part of the community.

"Let's take a peek inside Drucker's," said Judd. "I think you'll like it."

As Judd pushed opened the wood frame screen door, a little bell tinkled. Again, Rebecca was enchanted.

"I can't believe a place like this actually exists," she said.

The store was like an unopened time capsule. Yellow shoeprints painted on the pine plank floor led customers up and down the aisles. Against one wall wooden bins were brimming with penny candy. Above the bins, a handwritten sign said: *Please weigh and bag candy yourself.* Customers were responsible for writing down the correct price. It was the honor system. Even the cash register was an antique. It had been in continuous use since Drucker's opened in the 1940s.

Judd let The Woods mosey up and down the aisles while he filled a paper bag with pink and white *Good'n Plenties*. He glanced over at Dan and Rebecca. They were examining vintage post cards in a spinning wire rack.

Suddenly a shriek pierced the air.

Jesus! thought Judd.

It was the last thing he needed. Now what would the Woods' think?

Judd rushed to the door. Stan, Dan and Rebecca followed him.

The little girl on the mechanical turtle had somehow managed to flip over the side. She was dangling upside down from one of the stirrups while the turtle continued to buck back and forth.

"How do you turn this thing off!" said Judd, turning to Stan.

"I don't know," said Stan. "It always stops on its own when the coin runs out."

Judd looked down at the floor. An electrical cord ran from the base of the turtle to an outlet in the wall. With the toe of his topsider, Judd kicked the plug out. The bucking turtle rocked to a stop. Then Judd and Stan freed the girl from the tangled straps of the twisted stirrup.

"Are you okay?" asked Stan Drucker. "Are you hurt?"

The little Lupo girl wiped the tears off her cheeks and shook her head.

She was frightened, but she wasn't hurt.

"Come inside with me," said Stan. "Sometimes a little candy can help in a situation like this. Or maybe you'd rather have some ice cream? We just got in a fresh tub of mint chocolate chip – the green kind."

As Judd turned to The Woods, a delivery truck pulled up in front. The driver jumped out of the cab and walked toward the front porch of the general store. It was Michael Schneiderman, Editor-in-Chief of *The Turtleback Gazette*. Michael also delivered the paper to local vendors.

Michael waved.

"Howdy, Judd!" he called.

"Howdy, Mike," answered Judd.

Then Mike let fly a stack of newspapers tied in twine. They landed with a thud just inches from Judd's feet.

Judd looked down. The headline spanned the width of the front page. You'd have thought the *Titanic* had just sunk again.

TOWN SAYS NO TO LITTLE GIRL'S TOE

Beneath the headline was the reporter's by-line: written and researched by Marc Bozian.

Judd lifted his right foot and placed it back down on top of the headline.

"I don't think you've seen Bonds' yet," said Judd, shepherding the Woods away from Drucker's front porch.

"It's our local soda fountain," he explained, as he led the Woods across the street. "They make a milk shake that they call the *Awful-Awful* – because it's awfully big and it's awfully good. You've got to try it."

Rebecca Woods returned Judd's smile, but there was something different about it.

Chapter 4

Turtleback Lake June 2006

PEOPLE IN TURTLEBACK LAKE didn't worry about global warming. At least for the time being, it was working in their favor.

The "season" at Turtleback Lake was longer now. The water along the shoreline – if not in the depths of the unfathomably deep middle – was now warm enough to swim in from Memorial Day till well into September.

All of which was good for business.

When the weather was warm, daytrippers paid for passes to the beaches, families rented sailboats and canoes, and fishermen bought bait and tackle. At the restaurants and markets, sales doubled and tripled. And people who kept cabins and cottages as second homes made a pretty penny renting them out by the week, month or season.

It was one of these little rentals – a cabin on the lake's western shore – that had brought Deena Goode to Turtleback Lake in the first place.

It had been back in March or April when Deena spotted a tiny classified ad in the summer rental section of *The Bergen Record*. The headline, *"Piece of Paradise,"* caught her eye. The rest of the ad convinced her to call.

"Rustic log cabin on lakeshore in mountains of North Jersey," said the ad. *"Serene setting. Swim, fish, boat. Reasonable rent. Call owner."*

"Perfect," thought Deena. "Absolutely perfect."

It was exactly what Deena imagined she needed: a small desk by a window in a cabin overlooking a lake. In two months – three at most – the dissertation she had put off finishing for years would be done.

Deena dialed the number.

"You're the first caller," said the man on the other end of the line. "It's yours if you want it."

Deena asked him the rent. She could hardly believe her ears.

"I'll take it," she said, afraid that if she hesitated for even a moment someone else would snap it up.

"Sight unseen?" asked the man.

"Is there any reason why I shouldn't?" asked Deena.

The man hesitated. Should he tell her about…

"Forget it," said Deena, cutting off the man's silence. "I'll take it. When can I move in?"

They arranged for the lease to begin the second week in June, the day after the private school where Deena worked as a vice-principal let out for the summer.

Deena's only regret was that their conversation had ended so quickly. There was something about the man's voice – its timbre and his diction – that flicked some switch inside her. Then again, maybe it was best she'd gotten off the phone. Over the past twenty years, how many men had flicked that inner switch – and what had become of them?

This summer was going to be different. This summer there would be no men, no romance, and most of all, no sex. This summer she would allow no distractions.

* * *

Turtleback Lake was less than a hundred miles from Deena's condo in Edgewater, but it felt more like a thousand. She could hardly believe her eyes. Where did all these tree-covered mountains come from? She had lived in New Jersey all her life but she had never seen anything quite like this.

Deena pulled her Volvo into the clearing in front of the little cabin. When she hopped out she took the deepest breath she had taken in years. Instantly, she felt more alive. There was something in the air here.

She looked at the cabin. It was perched on a rise that sloped gently down to the water. Deena marveled that the cabin was made of real logs – logs that had once been trees, trees that had probably once stood in the very same clearing where she was standing now.

This was a far cry from the vinyl siding she had known all her life.

* * *

In the week that followed, Deena settled into a new routine. She rose with the sun and was at the little wooden table by the window, writing, by 6:30. Except to get up for a cup of coffee or to go to the bathroom, she worked straight through until one o'clock.

But it almost seemed wrong to call it 'work.' Sitting at the little wooden table with a pen in her hand, Deena would look up and gaze out the window. The strange white rock out in the middle of the lake mesmerized her. She'd stare at it and fall into a kind of trance. Then, breaking free of its hold, she'd start to write – and write and write. Never before had thoughts and ideas organized themselves so clearly in her mind. Never before had sentences poured so freely from her pen.

Deena laid her right hand on the stack of papers that were rising at the corner of her desk. Then she looked back out at the bleached white rock in the middle of the lake.

"Ah, my silent muse," she murmured. "Thank you."

Then, at one o'clock, with the sun high in the sky, Deena stopped. Her mind was best in the morning. And by one she was hungry.

As she made herself lunch, Deena thought how strange it was having no one to talk to. She had always been a talker, a gabber. Now she was thinking that maybe she had talked too much. Everything she had ever said in conversation, no matter how clever or insightful, just went *poof.* Words were uttered and then they were gone. And to whom had she been talking? *Men.* Men, who all turned out to be interested in one thing. And it wasn't the brilliance of her conversation.

But none of that mattered now. Deena had turned a corner and she wasn't going to turn back. She had set her sights on a goal: two little letters in front of her name. A capital *D,* and a small *r,* period. She knew plenty of women who actively pursued doctors. She, on the other hand, was going to become one. Dr. Goode. Dr. Deena Goode. It had a nice ring to it.

And all she had to do was finish her dissertation. And every day she was getting closer.

Deena took her lunch over to the window. Each day it was the same: an open-faced liverwurst and onion sandwich and a bottle of Carlsburg beer. It was a man's lunch – no different from what her grandfather had eaten back in the old country – but Deena liked it. When she was finished, she stripped naked and changed into a sleek, black, one-piece bathing suit. She walked barefoot down to the lake, took a few steps in from shore, then plunged in headfirst. She was a strong swimmer and the forty or fifty yards to the floating dock was nothing to her.

When she reached the dock, she pulled herself up onto its sun-warmed surface. Over the years, people had carved their initials into the weathered wood. *BL. OH. IA.* Who were these people and when had they been here? Then Deena let her fingers slip into the deep grooves that formed the initials *AA.* The man she was renting her cabin from was named August Andersen. *AA.* Remembering his voice on the phone, Deena rolled over onto her back and started to daydream. Steam rose from her body as the sun dried her suit.

Soon, the sun and the lapping water lulled Deena to sleep. She hadn't taken an afternoon nap since she was in kindergarten. It was a lifetime ago. Where had all those years gone?

Whatever dreams she was having made her toss and turn.

Meanwhile, far across the lake, a man on the lake's mountainous eastern shore was watching her through a pair of high-powered binoculars.

A few days earlier the man had been out on his deck when he spotted someone swimming near the lake's western shore. It was too far for him to make out who it was, but it appeared to be a woman. His curiosity was aroused. The swimmer seemed to have come down from the old Andersen cabin. When the swimmer climbed up onto the dock, the man went back inside his house for a pair of binoculars he had picked up at a garage sale at Coach

Lupo's a few years earlier.

The binoculars were powerful. They brought the woman so close he felt he could practically reach out and touch her. And looking at the steaming black bathing suit that clung to her body, he wanted to.

The man was a professional. He prided himself for always being available to his clients at their convenience. But now he found himself making excuses.

"No, I'm sorry," he would say. "I can't meet between 1:30 and 3:00."

The best he could do for them now was any time before 1:00 or after 3:15.

"Would that work?"

Russ Meyer, the mayor of Turtleback Lake, stood on a stage hung with red, white, and blue bunting. A crowd of hundreds was gathered on the green before him. His amplified voice came crackling through loudspeakers mounted to poles at the corners of the stage.

"Everybody thinks that turtles are slow," began the mayor. "But as the young people of our town have proved – on land and in the water – the turtles from this neck of the woods are anything but."

Mayor Meyer paused to clear phlegm from his throat with a cough. Then he continued.

"The runners on our track team take top honors, year in, year out. Our swimmers leave the competition in their wake. And as for our turtles, well, I think I'll let our turtles' speed speak for itself. And so, without further ado, boys and girls, please place your turtles on the starting line."

Dozens of children bent down and placed the turtles they'd been holding on a white chalk line that had been drawn across the green.

"On your mark...get set..."

BANG!

Deena was a half-block away but the sharp crack of the starter's pistol made her jump.

Deena had walked into town to get groceries for the coming week. Everywhere she looked there seemed to be a poster or banner heralding the town's 50th Annual Turtle Trot. Now, as she collected herself from the shock of the gun blast, Deena glanced in the direction from which it had come. She saw the large crowd gathered on the green.

For weeks now, Deena had kept her interactions to a minimum. It wasn't because she was unfriendly. If anything, she was the opposite. She just wanted to stay focused on what she was here for. And she had succeeded. Though cordial to shopkeepers, she had as yet to divulge her name to a single person. And she liked it that way. She liked being the mysterious stranger.

But now her curiosity was piqued. What was happening over on the village green?

Deena made her way to the edge of the crowd then started slipping through the throng of tightly packed bodies. Soon she had wriggled and squirmed her way to the second row. Only one person – a tall, broad-shouldered man – was left blocking her view.

"Excuse me!" she said, addressing the back of the man's head.

Either he didn't hear her, or he was choosing to ignore her.

"Excuse me!" she said again, louder.

Still the man didn't respond.

The crowd was going wild. Deena was afraid she'd miss whatever it was that they were cheering about. So she made her first contact with a native. She tapped the man in front of her on the shoulder.

Still he ignored her. So Deena tapped again, this time harder. The man remained completely impassive. Finally, she couldn't take it any longer. She had to do something, so she straightened her index finger and gave the man a good poke in the back.

At the same instant, the crowd roared and surged. Deena was thrust up against the man's back. The side of her face – her cheek, lips, and nose – was squished up against him. She could feel the heat radiating from his body. Then the man swung about abruptly, brushing against her breasts. Deena's last jab had hurt. The man was angry as he turned. But when he saw Deena his anger vanished.

"Oh," he said. "Hi! It's you."

"Do I know you?" asked Deena.

"No," said Judd, making room so Deena had a clear view of the turtles that were rumbling across the green toward the finish line. "I don't believe we've met. My name is Judd Clayton."

"Well, hi," she said. "My name's Deena – Deena Goode. Could you tell me what all this excitement's about?"

"It's a turtle race," said Judd. "Turtles are big around here. This race goes back fifty years."

"Hmm," said Deena.

The first turtle was about to cross the finish line when Judd leaned down to speak into Deena's ear. Then somebody in the crowd bumped against him. For a brief instant, he lost his balance and his lips brushed against Deena's ear.

"I'm so sorry," he said.

"Don't worry," said Deena. "It's nothing."

But it wasn't *nothing*. She and Judd both had tingled at the lip-to-ear contact.

As Russ Meyer handed out ribbons to the winners, the crowd started to disperse.

"Well, thanks for the play-by-play," said Deena. "But I better get going. I've got some shopping to do."

Deena turned to go. Judd reached out and took her by the arm. He couldn't let her escape.

"Please," he said. "Won't you join me for a cup of coffee over at Bonds'?"

Deena looked up at Judd. His fingers were wrapped around her forearm like a handcuff – or a bracelet. He was tall, fair-haired, blue-eyed. She was petite, raven-haired, olive skinned. A cup of coffee with him was the last thing she needed.

"All right," she said. "Just a quick cup."

* * *

"So," said Deena, after the waitress took their order, "back there on the green – when you first saw me – you said, 'It's you!' – like you already knew me."

Judd was afraid this was going to come up. It had been a real blunder, but it had slipped out before he could catch himself. Now what could he tell her?

"Well," said Judd. "I guess I could tell you I mistook you for somebody. Or..."

"Yes," said Deena. "Or?"

"Or," said Judd. "I could tell you the truth."

"Why don't we go with '*b*'," said Deena.

Judd knew it was a gamble. He took a deep breath. He'd tell her the truth – or at least part of it.

"It wasn't the first time I saw you," he said.

"Oh, really?" said Deena, her brown eyes widening. "When else have you seen me?"

Judd looked her straight in the eye. Their coffees had come, and Deena was drawing hers near, as if trying to protect a valuable chess piece. The game was on.

"I've seen you," said Judd. "In the lake."

"Really?" said Deena. "Then why haven't I seen you?"

"I can see you from my house," said Judd. "I live on the opposite shore."

"You must have pretty eyes," said Deena.

Judd smiled and blushed.

"Thank-you," he said.

Deena could've kicked herself. What a Dodo brain! 'You must have pretty eyes!' Or was it simply a Freudian slip – the real truth rushing to the surface?

"I meant to say, you must have pretty *good* eyes," said Deena. "The opposite side of the lake is pretty far away."

Deena studied Judd closely. He did have beautiful eyes. But they were behind a pair of lenses set in Georgio Armani frames. How could a man who wore glasses possibly have made out who she was from the other side of the lake?

Judd took a sip of his coffee. He swallowed. *Here goes*, he thought.

"I use binoculars," he said.

Deena continued to look into Judd's eyes.

"Can you blame me?" asked Judd with a little smile and a tilt of his head.

Deena shook her head from side to side. She had to give him credit: at least he had told her the truth. How many guys ever did that?

And it was true – Judd had told the truth. At least he had told what had been the truth. For the truth had evolved. The binoculars, strong as they were, hadn't brought the woman on the dock close enough. Judd had wanted to bring her even closer. So he had rummaged through his attic until he found a telescope he'd given to JJ as a birthday present years before. It was so the boy could observe the moon, the stars, and other heavenly bodies.

And as far as Judd was concerned, no body was more heavenly than Deena's – especially as she lay flat on her back in a wet bathing suit on a hot deck bobbing on the surface of Turtleback Lake.

Chapter 5

Turtleback Lake September 2006

MAYOR RUSS MEYER made the announcement at a special meeting of the Turtleback Lake Town council: The town would not dredge the lake in the area of the public beach in order to search for Joanne Sully's missing toe.

The council's decision was based on a number of factors.

"I have been advised by medical experts," said the mayor, "that reattachment surgery offers little hope in cases where the severed limb has been separated from a body for more than 48 hours."

Mayor Meyer let this important piece of information sink in.

"The likelihood of finding such a small body part," he continued, "in such a large body of water, within such a short period of time, is exceedingly low."

The mayor paused before adding the clincher.

"Furthermore, the cost of dredging would have to be paid for with funds from a budget that is already strained. Dredging," he concluded, "would be expensive, impractical, and ultimately useless."

"What do you say, Chief?" called out Jack Sully, a non-council member in attendance.

Police Chief Rudolph turned to face Jack.

"I think that toe could be anywhere now," he said. "It could be in the belly of whatever it was that bit your little girl. Or, if it's not there, it might've been swallowed by some pike or pickerel or who knows what."

"Oh, come on, Chief, we can't just do nothing," said Jack. "What if it were your kid?"

"It'd make no difference," said Chief Rudolph. "The odds of finding that toe are higher for a fisherman than for any dredging company we could hire. I'm sorry, Jack."

Meanwhile, Joanne Sully was miles away, in a bed at Northern Ramapo Hospital. The little girl might want to think twice about wearing open-toed shoes in the future, but other than that, she'd be just fine.

Certainly she wouldn't be the first or only resident of Turtleback Lake to be missing part of an extremity.

Two hundred over ninety.

And that was on a good day.

Bill Lupo's blood pressure was elevated to start. But the constant aggravation of his chosen occupation only pushed it higher. Hardly an hour in his life passed without someone infuriating him with one thing or another.

Receivers who slanted in instead of out. Guards who forgot to pull. Linebackers who missed tackles. Running backs who didn't seem to know the difference between the two hole and the four hole. Throw in school administrators, parents who complained about how much playing time their kids were getting, gym classes, and driver's ed, and you had a man ready to blow like Vesuvius.

Bill would probably already have been laid out in Schlemm's Funeral Home if it hadn't been for Sunday mornings. While others settled into creaking pews, Bill sat peacefully in a rowboat, a congregation of one.

Out on the lake with nothing but a rod and reel, Bill became another man. Catching something was beside the point. Here there was no one to give him *agita*.

And this Sunday morning was especially good. This Sunday morning Turtleback Lake had offered up its one true delicacy – a lovely, sixteen-inch lake trout. Trout were the only fish Bill kept. The rest – the large and small mouth basses, the perches and pickerels, the sunnies, blue gills, and pikes – all went back into the lake to catch again another day. But a trout like this one, silvery and speckled, with plump, delicate flesh, such a fish was meant to swim in a pan of melted, bubbling butter.

Bill knew that when he got back to shore, his daughter Mimi and his granddaughter Lulu would be waiting for him. They always came for Sunday morning brunch. But the rolls and cold cuts Bill had bought for their visit would have to wait. Today, they'd all be having fresh-caught lake trout.

For a moment, it actually felt good to be alive. Bill dipped his oars into the water. He couldn't wait to get to shore and show his catch to his daughter.

Then the oar in Bill's right hand jerked. Something was tugging at the end of it. The oar slipped out of his hand, swung wildly and struck Bill in the mouth, splitting his lip. He grabbed the oar again with two hands and pushed down hard. Using the gunwale as a fulcrum, he attempted to leverage up whatever was at the other end. The glare on the lake's surface was too bright for him to see what was beneath.

"*Damn!*" he muttered.

Whatever had hold of his oar was heavy.

Bill stood up to get better leverage.

Then he slipped and fell. The small wooden boat rocked violently. The back of Bill's head slammed against the side. Now he'd have an egg-size lump to go with his fat lip. Bill was sprawled across the bottom of the boat when he noticed the end of the oar suspended in the air. The wood was splintered, as if it had been thrust into a wood chipper. For a brief moment, Bill's mind flashed back to a night almost forty years earlier – the night he and his friend Oscar had tried paddling out to Turtleback Rock.

Bill peered into the water. A large dark form seemed to pass beneath the boat, but he couldn't be sure. It could've been the shadow of a cloud passing in front of the sun. All he knew for sure was that the oar in his hands was now useless.

Rowing back to shore with one good oar would be no piece of cake.

* * *

"Honey – I've fished that lake for fifty years and I've never seen anything like it."

Bill had just walked into the kitchen carrying the mangled oar.

"Whatever did this has gotta be one helluva snapper," he said, showing the oar's ravaged edge to his daughter.

Mimi Lupo wasn't particularly interested in the oar or her father's musings. She had her own story to tell. Little Lulu's tumble off the turtle in front of Drucker's was big news in her life. In a private corner of her mind she was secretly pondering the possibility of a lawsuit. Now she was being pre-empted by a broken oar and a trout.

"Clean this, will you, baby doll," her dad asked, slapping the trout onto the kitchen counter.

Mimi Lupo certainly didn't have the smarts to be a doctor. High school had been the end of the line for her, but still, she could clean a fish with the efficiency of a surgeon.

While little Lulu watched a DVD in the living room, and Bill sat puzzling over his oar, Mimi slit the ventral side of the trout from cloaca to gullet. The contents of its alimentary canal spilled out onto the cutting board.

Through the translucent membrane of the trout's distended belly, Mimi glimpsed something that looked vaguely human. She leaned in closer for a better look.

"Oh my God! Daddy!"

"What is it, baby?" said Bill, putting down the splintered oar and rising from his chair.

Bill walked over to the kitchen counter. There – inside the belly of his beautiful trout – was Joanne Sully's toe. The nail was painted pink.

The Snappers were the pride of Turtleback Lake. Over the years, the team had won sixteen conference championships, and the display case in the high school's front hall provided the gold-plated proof.

But beneath the surface, under the varsity jackets and thick letter sweaters, a darker truth lurked. Members of the team were given special license. They got away with stuff. They made underclassmen take back their trays in the cafeteria. They made smart kids do their homework. And they did other things that were even worse. But everyone looked the other way. You didn't mess with success. And for decades, The Snappers had been a powerhouse.

For freshman players, the first few weeks of September were a rude awakening. Even those whose had gone to Snapper games all their lives weren't prepared for what was to come. Towns had secrets – and the residents of Turtleback Lake kept theirs. There were things that no one knew about until it was their time to know.

The posted hours of Ted Tanner's Pet and Turtle Shop were 9 a.m. to 6 p.m. Now it was 8:30 p.m. and the sign hanging in the shop's darkened door said –

SORRY, CLOSED. PLEASE CALL AGAIN.

The streetlamp in front of the store barely illuminated the side alleyway where a group of teenage boys moved through the shadows, making their way to the back of Ted Tanner's store.

There was no light in back, and when Barry Calabrese bumped into a garbage can, its lid fell to the pavement and clattered like a cymbal.

"Willya watch where you're goin', *ya putz!*" hissed Savarese.

Savarese rapped on the back door. A minute later, the door cracked open an inch. A single eye peered out.

Ted Tanner scrutinized the faces of the boys gathered at his backdoor. He'd known most of them since they were toddlers. He'd sold them their first gold fish, their first pet turtles, their first aquariums. Now he would serve them in a different capacity.

"C'mon in, boys," he whispered.

The boys, eager to comply, all tried to squeeze through the doorway at once.

"Quit being such *stunods!*" snarled Savarese, shoving them forward from the rear.

They were in a narrow hallway at the back of the store. The only light came from a single light bulb screwed into the ceiling of a tiny bathroom. Through its half-closed door, the boys could hear the *drip, drip, drip* of a spigot. It had been dripping for twenty years.

"Watch your step, boys, we're going down," said Ted, "to the basement."

Descending the darkened stairs, JJ heard something besides the boys' clunking boots. It was a scraping, scuffling kind of noise, like wooden blocks being brushed and tapped together. There was also a foul smell, like animal waste mixed with dampness. But JJ couldn't see a thing. The basement was pitch black.

"Just keep moving," said Ted. "Keep your hands on the railing. When you reach the bottom, move aside and make room for the others."

Groping in the dark, JJ bumped into a teammate. He started to tumble. He put out his foot to stop his fall. But his foot didn't come down onto the flat concrete floor that he expected. It landed on something hard, curved, and slippery – like a wet rock.

Ted Tanner didn't have to see the string dangling from the overhead light bulb to find it. He reached up into the blackness, grabbed the string, and pulled.

The sudden glare blinded the boys. They reached up to cover

their eyes. They squeezed their eyelids shut, trying to squint away the pear-shaped image branded onto their retinas. It took almost a minute before they were able to look around and see where they were.

Now JJ understood why Ken Lubowsky had told him to wear work boots – *"with steel toes if you've got 'em."*

The basement floor of Ted Tanner's Pet and Turtle Shop was crawling with hundreds of snapping turtles.

"It's just like when you go to Max's Sea Shanty," said Ted, looking around at the boys who stood frozen as the turtles climbed over their boots and rubbed against their ankles.

"You know how they got that big tank up front – the one where you get to pick out your own lobster?"

The boys all nodded, even those who'd never been to Max's.

"It's the same deal here," said Ted. "You get to pick out the turtle you want. Only difference is, here you gotta grab it and kill it yourself. Makes him yours, if you know what I mean."

This was more than JJ had bargained for when Ken Lubowsky, the Snapper's starting halfback, had told him that afternoon that there was going to be a secret team meeting for freshmen players at eight-thirty.

"My dad's gonna wanna know where I'm going," said JJ.

"Make up some excuse," Ken had told him. "Tell him you're going to the library to study."

"But the library closes at six," JJ had said.

"Then make something else up," said Ken. "Tell him anything. Just be there."

JJ wasn't used to lying to his dad. It was something he'd never done. Every alibi he came up with seemed false and phony. As evening drew near, JJ began feeling almost sick. Then his dad called up from the bottom of the stairs.

"Hey, JJ! I was thinking about catching a movie at the Rialto tonight. Wanna come?"

JJ thanked God.

"I can't, Dad," he called. "Too much homework."

"Mind if I go?" asked Judd. "You'd be alone for a couple of hours."

It was perfect. The Rialto was on the other side of the mountain, at least thirty minutes away. There and back would take an hour, plus the length of the movie. JJ would have three hours plus. How long could a team meeting last?

"I'll be fine," said JJ. "Have a good time."

* * *

"So," said Savarese, glowering at the boys in Tanner's basement. "Who's going to be first?"

No one answered.

"No problem," said Savarese. "I'll get the ball rolling. *Mars man* – you're up first."

"*Mars man*" was Ricky Marsten, a gawky, six-foot kid who had hoped his height would make him a good target as a pass receiver.

"How am I supposed to grab one," he asked, "without getting bit?"

"From behind," said Ted Tanner. "Like this."

Tanner bent down and plucked a turtle from the writhing mass on the basement floor.

The turtle craned its head and neck. It thrashed with its front paws and snapped violently at the air, but neither its blade-like jaw nor its razor-sharp claws could reach Ted Tanner's fingers.

"It's easy," he said.

As the angry snapper hissed in the glare of the naked bulb, JJ observed something he'd never noticed before: The ring finger of Mr. Tanner's left hand was missing.

"C'mon, son, show some spunk!" said Mr. Tanner. "We haven't got all night!"

JJ wasn't the only player who had noticed Ted Tanner's missing digit. Ricky Marsten had seen it, too. Mr. Tanner had grabbed the turtle as though there was nothing to it, but the stump on his left hand made Marsten think there definitely had been a learning curve involved.

Marsten thought about his parents. If he lost a finger, eight years of piano lessons would go right down the drain. They wouldn't be happy.

"I can't do it," he said.

"Either you do it," said Savarese, "or you turn in your uniform tomorrow."

Marsten knew he was already less than nothing in Savarese's eyes. He couldn't redeem himself now. His moment of hesitation had marked him as a coward forever. He knew his football playing days were over. At least he'd still be able to play the piano. And face his parents.

"I'll drop my stuff off in Lupo's office tomorrow," he said.

No one said a word as Marsten clomped back up the basement steps and disappeared through the backdoor.

"All right," snarled Savarese. "Who's next?"

During the next hour, two boys followed in Ricky Marsten's footsteps, three boys received nasty bites that Tanner stitched up without anesthesia, and two dozen snapping turtles were caught and killed.

When JJ's turn came, he did as the boys before him had done. After grabbing a turtle, he drove tacks through its limbs to pin it on its back. Then he placed the tip of a six-inch nail against the turtle's hard undercarriage. Then, he lifted a hammer above his head and with one ferocious blow drove the nail through the turtle's plastron and heart.

When the turtle finally stopped twitching, Tanner gave JJ a long, pointed knife and instructed him on the art of cleaning a turtle. Using the knife's serrated edge, JJ sawed through the wrinkly, leathery hide and tough, sinewy ligaments that connected the turtle to its carapace and plastron.

Then, using something that looked like an oversized grapefruit spoon, JJ scooped out the turtle's guts. The slop of bloody innards was sloughed off the edge of the table into a large metal pot.

When the turtles all had been butchered, and each shell tagged with a player's number, Savarese addressed his teammates.

"Tonight, each of you has made a major step toward becoming a true Snapper. The shell of the turtle you caught, killed, and cleaned, will be baked dry and enameled. It will become your shell, the armor protecting your manhood, in our battles on the gridiron."

Savarese glowered at the remaining boys. Then, at a nod from Mr. Tanner, Savarese thrust his right hand deep into the crotch of his pants and withdrew a cup.

It wasn't a store-bought plastic cup like the one he had pulverized in front of JJ's locker.

It was the kiln-fired shell of a snapper that he had killed in the same ceremony three years earlier. Over the decades, who knew how many snappers had met the same fate?

Ted Tanner. Ted Tanner knew. He was the keeper of the book – a deathlog in which Ted kept a running count of every snapper ever killed.

"Oh, and one last thing," said Savarese. "We'll be having our Freshman Team Dinner on Friday. You're going to love it. Especially if you like homemade turtle soup."

A week passed without a word from the Woods.

Jack and Janet Jensen were getting nervous. Judd had told them he was sure that the Woods were "this close" to making an offer. So what was the problem?

For three straight days the Jensens called Judd. On the third day they demanded he call the Woods. "Look," said Judd. "It's best not to appear too needy."

"We don't care how it appears," said Jack. "Just call them and see what's happening."

"All right," said Judd. "I'll call."

Rebecca Woods was tying up newspapers when the phone rang. She answered without checking to see who it was.

"Hi, Rebecca. It's me – Judd Clayton. I just thought I'd touch base."

Rebecca said nothing for two or three seconds. Judd knew it was a bad sign. Rebecca was clearly couching her reply.

"We liked everything you showed us, Judd," said Rebecca, "especially the Jensen house. But we've decided it's just not the right fit for us."

Judd knew it was a lost cause. Still he couldn't help himself. He kept on selling.

"I know the house is pretty pricey," he said. "But I think the Jensens' might be willing to bend a bit."

"That's nice, Judd," said Rebecca, "but it's not really a matter of price."

"If it's not price," said Judd, "could you tell me what it is? You and Dan both seemed so excited."

Rebecca kicked herself for taking the call. She should have let it go through to voice mail. This was a conversation she definitely did not want to be having.

"Judd, I don't know quite how to put it," said Rebecca. "It's hard to put a finger on. It's really more of a feeling than anything else."

Good salesmen know when to stop selling. Judd knew he'd already gone too far. He stopped himself now.

"Well, I certainly respect your decision, Rebecca," said Judd. "And if you change your mind, or if I can help you in any way in the future, please don't hesitate to call."

Six percent of a million – *sixty thousand dollars* – had just slipped through his fingers.

It was bad, but it was far worse for the Jensens'. And he was the messenger. *Oh, well,* thought Judd, *it goes with the territory.*

As Judd dialed the Jensens', Rebecca Woods finished tying up her newspapers. They were all *New York Times* and *Wall Street Journals* – except for the one on top. It was a *Turtleback Gazette.*

Rebecca glanced down at the headline one last time as she carried the papers out to the recycling bin. Once again Michael Schneiderman had used a Titanic-size font for the headline. Sales surged whenever he did.

MISSING TOE FOUND IN TROUT

In the upper right hand corner of the front page, Michael Schneiderman also had added the paper's newly-coined slogan: *Stories That Change Lives.*

Every September, it was the same. Students at Turtleback High added, dropped, or switched classes like crazy. The person next to you one day could be gone forever by the next; you might never get to know them.

The girl sitting next to JJ in Biology disappeared before the teacher even knew her name. For a few days, her desk remained empty.

Then one morning as Mr. Martinetti was diagramming cells on the blackboard, the classroom door swung open and a girl walked in.

Mr. Martinetti turned from the blackboard and waited as she walked toward him. All eyes were on her. She seemed used to it; anyone that pretty would have to be.

Mr. Martinetti was young – just a few years out of college. He couldn't help eyeballing the girl as she handed him her transfer form.

"Welcome to the class," he said, looking over her form. "Take any desk that's available."

JJ's heart started to race. There were plenty of desks available. JJ's desk – and the empty desk next to him – was in the front row. His father had told him, "If you really want to learn something, sit in the front." Most kids headed straight for the back.

A roomful of eyes watched to see where the pretty blonde girl would sit. She looked around the room then walked straight toward the empty desk in the first row.

As she seated herself, JJ smelled the shampoo she had used that morning. He knew it because he used it himself. It was Herbal Essence.

Mr. Martinetti turned back to his cell diagram. His chalk clicked against the blackboard as he drew in tiny specks that represented something he said was "mitochondria."

The new girl leaned toward JJ and chanted in the softest whisper, *"Hey, ho, twenty-four, haven't I seen you before?"*

Chapter 6

Turtleback Lake 1928

Turtles can live a long time.

Their sense of time is different from ours. They feel no compulsion to act rashly. They can wait. They've got staying power.

Grundel was already in his thirties when Isaac Andersen pissed on his back. Grundel didn't like it. He had pursued the boy through tangles of branches and underbrush, plowing through them like a tank.

It was dark in the woods but that didn't matter. Grundel spent huge parts of his life in blackness that was wet and cold. At least here there was the spectral glow of the moon filtering through the crosshatch of leaves and branches above. As he plowed forward, Grundel saw another light: the hot flickering flames of a campfire. That was where Grundel would have his revenge. He would teach the boy a lesson. He was not a child's urinal. He would take a toe, a finger, a foot or a hand – whatever presented itself. He would have his revenge and that would be that. He simply would snap and sever, then take his booty back to the lake. No one would piss on him again.

In the clearing by the fire, Owen Andersen couldn't make out why Isaac was so frantic. He had only been gone for two minutes and now he was back, blubbering incoherently.

"Calm down, Isaac," said Owen. "Just tell me what happened."

The words blurted out of Isaac's mouth.

"I was peeing – peeing on a rock and it started getting bigger and bigger – and then it came charging – charging out of the water!"

"Isaac, calm down," his father said again. "A rock can't charge out of the water."

"It wasn't a rock, Dad, it was…"

Isaac stopped in the middle of his sentence. Grundel had suddenly burst into the clearing.

Owen Andersen immediately dropped the soapy utensils in his hands. He glanced around for something – anything – he could use as a weapon. He reached for the first thing he saw: the long, wood-handled ax that he and Isaac used to chop down trees for the cabin they were building.

Owen stood with his feet a yard apart, holding the ax like a baseball player waiting for a pitch.

Grundel charged across the clearing. Owen waited till the beast was in his strike zone, then he swung. The heavy steel ax head sliced through the air and struck Grundel's shell. The blade sank into the horny carapace. Owen tried to free it for a second swing, but he couldn't. The blade was wedged deep in the giant turtle's back. Owen yanked at the handle and his feet went out from under him. He tumbled backwards onto the ground by the fire.

Grundel turned his head toward the man, hissing with rage

and pain. He eyed the man malevolently, then his body shot forward, his great beak gaping open. Owen raised an arm to protect his face and throat.

The first chomp did not completely sever the hand. It cut through flesh, muscles, and veins, but only got halfway through the ulna. Without letting go, Grundel gave his jaw another squeeze. This time the hand clipped clean. Grundel clenched the detached limb in his mandible. Owen Anderson's fingers stuck out like nails from a carpenter's mouth.

Grundel turned. His eyes swept over the boy. The boy stood frozen. He was trembling, with saltwater tears streaming down his face. *Forget the boy,* Grundel thought: *I have the hand of the father.*

Grundel clawed his way back toward the lake. The return trip was harder. The long handle of the ax jutting out from his back kept getting snagged in the twigs and branches overhead.

Chapter 7

Turtleback Lake September 2006

TRIMMED IN DARK FEDERAL GREEN and sided in white clapboard, Clayton Realty was as charming as any storefront in downtown Turtleback Lake.

But what made it a magnet – what really stopped people as they passed by – were the houses pictured and described in its windows. No one could resist stopping to see which homes were on the market and how much they were going for. Over the last decade, real estate had become Turtleback Lake's most lucrative industry.

Judd couldn't remember the last time he'd put a Price Reduced sticker on a home. It had to have been back in the nineties. But now the Jensens' wanted one on theirs.

When the season was just starting back in May, Judd practically had guaranteed the Jensens' that they'd get their asking price – and probably thousands more.

But that was before the turtle attacks. Whatever Dr. Goode might have said to the contrary, the snapper situation in Turtleback Lake had definitely become an issue. And it wasn't going to go away – especially with guys like that young reporter, Marc Bozian, stirring up trouble.

Looking out his office window, Judd saw Michael Schneiderman dropping off a stack of newspapers on Drucker's front porch. Judd rose from his desk and hurried across the street. He wanted a word with Mike.

"Look, Mike," Judd began. "I'm not saying you shouldn't report on things like this little girl's toe. But don't you think those TITANIC-size headlines are a bit over the top?"

Michael eyed Judd before answering. He was tempted to tell Judd that his paper's newsstand sales had more than doubled and that he'd gotten requests for twenty new subscriptions in the last week alone, but that might give Judd the wrong impression. Increased circulation wasn't the goal of good journalism. It was just a happy by-product.

"I see your point, Judd," said Michael. "But people have a right to know the facts. Swimming in the lake could be dangerous."

"But what facts do we really know, Mike?" said Judd. "The way people are talking, you'd think the lake was stocked with piranhas. For chrissakes, people are even bringing up that old myth about a giant snapper. This Bozian guy is making it seem like we've got a Loch Ness Monster up here. It's not good for the town, Mike. Just look."

Judd reached down and pulled out a *Turtleback Gazette* from the stack at his feet. He opened it to the real estate page.

"Look," he said. "Just look at all those priced reduced signs. People are dropping their prices right and left."

Michael said nothing.

"Listen, Mike," said Judd. "You don't want this Bozian guy to drag the whole town under – do you?"

Mike shook his head. He understood Judd's position. And he was glad that he wasn't trying to sell his own home at this time.

On the other hand, it wouldn't be a bad time to buy.

Chapter 8

Turtleback Lake June 2006

DEENA HAD MIXED FEELINGS about her cup of coffee with Judd. When they left Bonds', Judd offered her a ride back to her cabin.

"Thanks, but no," said Deena. "I've got some shopping to do."

"I'd be glad to wait," said Judd.

He sensed Deena was wavering.

"Just so you don't have to carry the bags all the way back yourself," said Judd.

Deena still thought she should say no. But what she said was, "Okay, sure, if you don't mind."

A half hour later, when they pulled up in front of Deena's cabin, Judd popped the trunk. Then he hopped out and started lifting out Deena's bags of groceries.

"You know," said Judd, cradling three bags in his arms, "I've been inside almost every home in Turtleback Lake, but I've never been inside the Andersen cabin. Would you mind if I took a quick peek?"

Deena looked at the bags Judd was holding. They looked heavy.

"Sure," she said. "Why not?"

Once inside, Judd laid the three bags down on the kitchen counter. Then he walked over to the window and looked out toward the lake.

"Nice view," he said.

"I know," said Deena. "I've spent a lot of time looking out that window."

Deena started putting away groceries into the cabinets above the sink. She stood on the tips of her toes, but still it was difficult for her to reach. What she really needed was a step stool. Suddenly, Judd came up from behind her.

"Here," he said, taking a box of pasta from Deena's outstretched hand. "Let me help."

As Judd reached up, his body pressed against hers. The next moment, after placing the box of pasta on the top shelf, his arms enfolded her. Deena took a deep breath then let out a long sigh. She rotated slowly in Judd's arms till they were facing each other. She exhaled again and closed her eyes. Then she lifted up her chin, and offered her slightly parted lips to Judd.

Ten minutes later they were lying on the couch. Judd was in heaven. It had been years since he'd been with a woman.

"Wow!" he said, gazing at Deena's profile as she fixed her eyes on the ceiling. "You really are good."

Judd was sure that Deena would find his *double-entendre* clever: Goode, good.

But she didn't. She'd heard it before – too many times. And now that the passion was past, regret was moving in like a cold front. Why had she allowed Judd into her cabin?

"Is that your dissertation?" said Judd, pointing toward the stack of papers by the window.

After weeks of being alone, Deena had opened up too quickly back at Bonds'. She had even told Judd about her dissertation.

Now Judd rose from the couch and walked over to the table by the window.

"Mind if I take a look?" he asked, reaching toward the top sheet of paper.

Deena snapped bolt upright, pressing a pillow to her chest. "No!"

She hadn't meant to snap, but that's how it sounded. Judd turned, looking both startled and hurt.

"I'm sorry," he said. "I didn't mean to pry."

"No," said Deena. "I'm sorry. Forgive me. I didn't mean to sound so harsh. It's just that I don't want anyone to see it till it's finished."

A wave of jealousy swept over Judd. Deena had just given him her body. Now she wouldn't even let him take a peek at a pile of papers? He felt rejected. But then he remembered a little technique that he had learned in a realtor training class years before. Judd started counting slowly backwards from ten inside his head. By the time he reached zero, Judd was calm – or at least calmer.

"I'm truly sorry," he said. "I understand completely. Please forgive me."

"No," said Deena. "Forgive me. I overreacted."

* * *

The next morning, Deena was at her desk, shaking her head.

"*What* was I thinking?" she kept asking herself over and over. Work suddenly seemed impossible. The flow of words and ideas had stopped cold, as if a tap inside her head had been turned off. Instead of gazing out at the distant white rock in the middle of the lake, Deena found herself looking toward the far shore – at a house perched high up on the hillside. Judd had pointed it out to her the previous afternoon.

"That's my house," he had said. "That's where I live."

Deena could clearly see the windows of Judd's house from where she sat. And if she could see *his* windows, then surely he could see *hers*. With binoculars, he might even be able to see through them.

By noon, Deena had accomplished nothing. Her swim after lunch did nothing to lighten her dark mood. If anything, it made matters worse. Lying on her back out on the dock, Deena felt like an amoeba on a slide, magnified and scrutinized. She knew Judd was probably watching her. What was she supposed to do – sit up, smile, and wave?

Suddenly she felt an itch on the inside of her thigh. Yesterday she would have simply reached down and scratched herself. But today? With someone watching? It was just too much.

Finally, Deena couldn't stand it. She stood abruptly, dove into the lake, and swam back to shore almost as if she was being chased.

Since she'd been in Turtleback Lake, Deena hadn't written a single word after one o'clock. But since she'd wasted the entire morning, she decided she'd try. But thoughts of Judd kept intruding. Could he see her through her window? Was he watching her even now? Should she lower the blinds? But then she'd lose her beautiful view. And if she lowered the blinds, Judd would know she was shutting him out. He'd feel – what? *Spurned? Shunned? Rejected?*

Deena couldn't believe it! Here she was – trying to find the right word to describe how a man she'd met only yesterday *might* feel if she were to lower her blinds. It was insanity! It was exactly the kind of thing she'd come here to get away from.

This was not what she wanted. This was not what she had been doing every day until yesterday. Everything was ruined. She cursed Judd – and she cursed herself.

Then the phone rang.

It was the first time it had rung since she'd moved in

The ring was the old-fashioned kind – just what you'd expect from an old black rotary phone. The receiver was solid and heavy. Deena knew exactly how heavy because she'd been using it as a dumbbell, doing curls in her tank top while standing in front of the mirror.

Deena was as toned as a twenty-five-year old. She liked watching her biceps pop up every time she curled the receiver toward her shoulder. Ten, fifteen reps – just like the damn phone that was ringing now. Why didn't it stop? Who would keep ringing so long without getting an answer?

It *had* to be Judd – because he could *see* she was in. He probably was watching her right now as she debated whether or not to answer the phone.

Well, she would just give Mr. Judd Clayton a piece of her mind!

Deena picked up the receiver and pressed the earpiece against her right ear – the same ear that Judd had nibbled, then whispered into, the day before.

"Listen, you!" she snapped into the mouthpiece.

"Excuse me?" said a voice on the other end.

Deena caught herself. The voice on the line wasn't Judd's. It belonged to someone else – someone she had spoken to once before – and had wanted to speak to longer.

Chapter 9

Turtleback Lake 2005

When The Copelands' bought the Grants' house in Turtleback Lake's prestigious Skytop neighborhood, Judd Clayton handled the sale. He made a tidy sum. But he gained something he valued even more than his commission: a new best friend for his son.

Don and Ashley Grant had been nice neighbors, but they were older and their kids were long grown and gone. The Copelands', on the other hand, had a son, Ian, and though he was almost two years older than JJ, the two boys instantly hit it off. That first summer, JJ showed Ian all around Turtleback Lake. Together they spent the entire summer swimming, fishing, and biking. They canoed and kayaked. They spent hours playing on an old tire swing that sent them flying far out into the lake. They even liked the same kind of music, the same books, the same movies. The biggest difference between them was sports.

"What team are you going out for in the fall?" JJ asked.

"Soccer," said Ian. "What about you?"

"I'll still be just in eighth grade," said JJ. "But next year, when I'm a freshman, I'm going out for football."

"Yeah, well," said Ian. "I'm a soccer guy. I played it at my old high school."

When September came, Ian signed up for the soccer team. He stood out immediately. The balls Ian kicked were like missiles: they were targeted and they went further – much further – than anyone else's. One afternoon during the first week of school, Coach Lupo stood watching as Ian kicked a ball around the soccer field.

"Hey, Jenks," he said to his assistant. "Take over for a couple of minutes, okay? I've got something to check out."

"No problem, Bill," said Coach Jenkins. "Take your time."

Cradling a football in his hands, Coach Lupo strode straight toward Ian.

"Hey, son," he said, addressing the tall lanky kid he'd never seen before. "What's your name?"

"Ian Copeland."

"I don't think I've seen you around before," said Lupo. "You're not a freshman, are you?"

"No," answered Ian. "My family just moved here this summer. I'm a sophomore."

Coach Lupo gave the football in his hands a spin.

"Do you think you could kick this ball the way you've been kicking that one?" he asked, nodding toward the soccer ball at Ian's feet.

"I don't know," said Ian. "I've never tried."

"Well, I'd like you to give it a try," said Coach Lupo. "Come with me."

Coach Lupo took Ian by the arm and led him out onto the football field. They walked out to the 30-yard line. Coach Lupo got down on his knees, placed the ball on end, and held it upright at a slight angle with his forefinger.

"Think you can put it through those uprights?" he asked, indicating the white goal posts in the distance.

Ian shrugged. He took two quick strides toward the ball. His right leg swung forward and swept under the ball like a scythe. Spinning end over end, the ball sailed across the blue September sky and split the uprights, dead center.

The kick would've been good, with room to spare, from fifty yards.

Coach Lupo got up from his knees and placed his right hand on Ian Copeland's shoulder.

"You know, son," said Coach Lupo, "soccer is really more of a European sport."

The coach gave Ian a moment to digest this important fact. Then he continued. "Round here, the game we like to play is football. It's a good, old-fashioned American game. You'd be a real asset to the team."

"What about Coach Massari?" asked Ian.

"Don't worry about Bernie," smiled Lupo. "I'll explain everything to him."

* * *

Placekickers are a different breed. Nobody expects them to really fit in with the rest of the team.

The only thing anyone really cares about is how they kick. And that Fall, nobody in New Jersey kicked better than Ian Copeland. Ian's kickoffs eliminated runbacks. How could you return a kick that sailed out of the end zone? Ian's extra points were automatic. And every time the Snappers got within their opponents' 35-yard line, they were assured of putting at least three points up on the board.

Ian was cool and clutch. He also was remarkably clean. That whole first season, he got only one grass stain on his pants – when he was mobbed by his teammates and fell to the ground after providing the margin of victory as time expired in the conference championship game. It was the Snappers' sixteenth conference championship.

Still Ian remained a bit of an outsider. Transferring in as a sophomore, he had missed the freshman rite of passage at Ted Tanner's Pet and Turtle Shop. Ian never impaled a snapper with a six-inch nail, he never scooped out a snapper's guts with a serrated spoon, and he never ate homemade turtle soup.

And the cup snapped in the pouch of Ian's jockstrap was made of good, old-fashioned, store-bought American plastic.

Chapter 10

Turtleback Lake September 2006

But that was last year.

Ian was now a junior and JJ was a freshman. They were Snappers together.

Since practice had begun back in August, they had developed a routine. As soon as practice was done and they were back in street clothes, they'd hop on their bikes and race home. It was like a two-man *Tour de France*. The two boys sped neck and neck up into the hills that encircled Turtleback Lake. By the time they reached home, their chests were heaving and their skin was filmed with slick coats of sweat.

Then they'd dismount and run down to the lake for a swim.

Today though, practice had run late. It was practically seven when they got home. The sun was dropping below the mountains in the west. The sky had turned a pinkish orange. But the color wouldn't last long. At this time of the year, late September, darkness came on quickly. Still, the two boys were hot and sweaty from their bike ride.

"What do you think?" asked JJ. "We got time for a dip?"

"I don't know," said Ian. "It's late – and I've got a ton of homework."

Ian looked across the lake. The sky above the mountains was beautiful – like a Maxfield Parrish painting – but little of that light reached the lake. The surface of Turtleback Lake was dark, almost black. Only the strange white rock out in the middle seemed to catch any of the day's waning light. Ian didn't like to admit it, especially to someone who was two years younger, but swimming in the lake after sunset made him nervous. He knew it was irrational – it was the exact same lake after all – but still, there it was, the lake at night gave him the creeps.

"Oh, come on," said JJ. "We'll make it quick."

"All right," said Ian. "But just a quick one."

The boys raced down the wooden staircase that zigzagged down to the dock far below. The dock jutted out into the lake like a pier. At the end of it, Ian and JJ stripped down to their briefs and then plunged into the darkening water.

They didn't swim out too far. Each boy was seeking the same thing: one of the warm thermal updrafts that rose up here and there from the bottom of the lake. Turtleback Lake was famous for them.

"Find one?" JJ called out.

"Yup!" said Ian. "It feels great."

"Mine too," said JJ.

The two boys treaded with their arms and legs, keeping themselves in the columns of warm water. Only their heads and necks broke the surface.

"So," said Ian. "What's going on between you and Mary Robinson?"

"What are you talking about?" said JJ.

"Oh, come on, JJ! I'm not blind."

"Really, Ian, nothing's going on," insisted JJ. "Maybe she likes me a little – as a friend."

"And I suppose you just like her – as a friend?"

"I'd like to like her as more," said JJ. "But I don't think there's much of a chance of that."

"I don't know," said Ian. "That '*Hey ho, 24,*' stuff sounds like she might like you more than you think."

"Yeah, well," said JJ. "I guess I can dream."

As the boys talked, the sky in the west bruised from orangey pink to purplish black. In the east, a round white moon began rising like a balloon. And in the cold depths of Turtleback Lake, a dark domed form stroked and glided, moving ever closer to the two boys treading in their warm columns.

Grundel had suddenly felt drawn forth. The rising moon seemed to be summoning him. And as he rose from the depths towards the shallower waters along the eastern shore, his yellow eyes perceived two glowing shapes wiggling like white worms in the warm water. As he drew nearer, he took inventory: two lithe bodies, four legs and feet, four arms and hands, and ten, twenty, thirty, forty little fingers and toes! Grundel was delighted. His belly was empty. But it would not be for long.

Grundel eyed his two targets. He chose the one with the longest, lankiest limbs. They were Ian's – Ian's legs – including the one that sent footballs sailing through uprights. Like a jumbo jet banking in a liquid sky, Grundel tilted his body, adjusted the arc of his approach, and went in with his jaw wide open.

Oscar Hall had been the janitor at Turtleback High School longer than anyone could remember.

For almost four decades, he had walked up and down its tiled hallways, his left foot leading and his right foot dragging behind. For almost forty years, students had mocked and mimicked Oscar's limp – and not always behind his back.

Yet despite his infirmity, no one could match Oscar's ability to quickly fill a gymnasium with folding metal chairs.

For the emergency town meeting being held in the high school gym, Oscar had set up every chair available. Still there were not enough chairs for everyone. Those who didn't come early had to stand on the side or in the back. Others sat in the center aisle on the gym floor, a violation of fire code that Police Chief Rudolph chose to ignore.

Now it was 8:10. People were still squeezing in through the back door, but the meeting had been scheduled to start at eight and Chief Rudolph felt he'd waited long enough. He walked over to the podium and reached for the microphone.

"If I can please have your attention," he began.

The buzz of conversations continued unabated. It was as if no one had heard him. Chief Rudolph tapped – then cursed – the mike.

"Damn it!" he said. "This darn thing's not working. Where the hell is Oscar?"

Chief Rudolph looked to the left for some help from his deputy, Donald Rhodes, but Donny seemed wholly absorbed by a hangnail on the thumb of his left hand.

"Hey, for chrissakes, Donny, get me Oscar, double-quick!"

A minute later, Oscar emerged from the wings, dragging his right leg behind him as he limped toward the podium.

"This damn thing doesn't work, Oscar," said Chief Rudolph, thrusting the microphone toward him. "Can you find me another?"

Oscar took the microphone from Chief Rudolph's outstretched hand. He flicked a switch at the base of the handle. A sudden ear-splitting screech filled the room. Hundreds of people simultaneously reached up to cover their ears. They looked at Oscar and the Chief with pained and reproachful faces.

Oscar gave the orb at the top of the mike a quick twist and silenced the piercing noise. He handed the mike back to Chief Rudolph.

"It should work fine now, Rudy."

"Thanks, Oscar."

Chief Rudolph turned back to the crowd. The screeching mike had done the trick. He now had their undivided attention.

"Thank you all for coming tonight," he began. "There's been a lot of talk going around so I want to give you the facts as I know them. First, I want to let you know that the boy who was attacked in the lake last night, Ian Copeland, is in stable condition. He's at a hospital in the city where he's getting the best medical care available.

"I also want to acknowledge the actions of Ian's friend, JJ Clayton. Without JJ's quick response, things could've turned out much worse."

Chief Rudolph paused to clear his throat.

"Now, as to the cause of Mr. Copeland's grievous injury, I can only tell you that the only witness we have – JJ Clayton – says that immediately after the attack, something scraped against him underwater. Whatever it was, he said, felt rough, hard, and shell-like.

Furthermore, JJ received a number of lacerations that suggest the claws of a large aquatic predator."

A man in the middle of the crowd suddenly called out.

"What do you mean by 'a large aquatic predator?'"

"Just hold on," said Chief Rudolph. "All I can say is that based on the nature of the injuries – Ian Copeland's severed leg, the lacerations on JJ's torso, and JJ's description of whatever it was that scraped against him – when all these factors are taken into account, it seems reasonable to me that we can assume with some degree of certainty that what we are dealing with here is a *Chelydra Serpentina Magnus.*"

The crowd suddenly appeared confused and perplexed – like a class of students who no longer can follow what their teacher is saying.

Again, someone in the crowd called out.

"You want to translate that into English, Chief?"

"A *Chelydra Serpentina Magnus,*" repeated Chief Rudolph, not entirely confident with his pronunciation of a term he had just learned himself that day, "is the Latin, or scientific name, for a giant snapping turtle."

High school administrators keep the names and numbers of grief counselors handy for three simple reasons: Automobiles, alcohol, and adolescence. Each year, these three A's combine to rob high schools of hundreds of young lives.

Deena Goode – or Dr. Goode as it said on the nameplate on her desk – was in her office, flipping through past editions of *The*

Spectrum, the Turtleback High School yearbook. On the final page of several, she saw pictures of students who had not lived to graduate. In their photos, their young eyes burned bright with futures yet to come. Yet all were now dead, gone and buried. At seventeen.

Dr. Goode shook her head. She had not known any of these children. They were all before her time. Yet she had a close call on her hands now. Ian Copeland easily could have joined the roll call of the dead, though not because of drinking and driving, but because of whatever it was that was lurking in the lake.

Deena didn't think the current situation would require outside counselors. Ian hadn't died. But there was no denying there had been a loss. When she thought of the tall lanky boy without his right foot, she shuddered. It was too horrible to imagine.

The students in the hallways that morning had looked stunned, as if they'd been turned into zombies overnight. Nobody was talking. Everybody looked down at the ground, as if they were ashamed – or guilty – of something.

After a fitful night spent tossing and turning, JJ had come downstairs that morning to find Police Chief Rudolph waiting for him in the kitchen.

"I hate to bother you again, JJ," he'd said, "but I just want to go over a few things from last night one more time. Just to make sure we didn't miss anything."

By the time Chief Rudolph left, it was past ten.

"You've been through hell, JJ," said Judd. "Why don't you stay home today? I'll stay home with you."

"Thanks, dad," said JJ. "But no – I think I want to go."

JJ couldn't say why, but for some reason, he didn't want to stay home. He wanted to go to school, maybe to get the whole thing over with. What did his grandmother used to say? *Meet it, greet it, and beat it.*

As Judd pulled up in front of the high school, he asked JJ one last time.

"Are you really sure you want to go, JJ?"

JJ nodded.

"Don't worry, dad," he said. "I'll be fine."

JJ got out of the car and walked in through the front entrance. He walked past the glass case filled with trophies, then headed down the hall toward his locker. Students in the hallways parted as he approached. He felt like Moses walking through the Red Sea. Whenever JJ looked toward anyone, they dropped their eyes to the ground. Even Bobby Savarese looked down when JJ passed.

JJ opened the door to his biology class. The lesson had already started. Mr. Martinetti was at the blackboard again, this time drawing dendritic cells. He had planned to have a lab class today on paramecia, but he had changed his mind. Paramecia could grow back lost body parts. It seemed like the wrong day for a lesson on regeneration.

"Dendritic means tree-like," said Mr. Martinetti, looking up suddenly as JJ entered the room.

"I'm sorry I'm late," said JJ.

"Don't worry about it," said Mr. Martinetti.

Mary Robinson fixed her eyes on JJ the moment he entered the room. When their eyes finally met as he walked toward his desk, Mary held his gaze. As he sat down next to her, she reached over and covered his hand with hers.

"I'm so sorry about what happened, JJ," she said.

There were tears in her eyes.

She gave JJ's hand a squeeze. Then she pressed a small, folded square of paper into his palm.

Suddenly, the phone on the wall rang. Mr. Martinetti walked over and answered it.

"Hello," he said.

Then he looked up and glanced over at JJ.

"Yes," he said, into the receiver. "He's here."

A moment later, Mr. Martinetti hung up and turned to JJ.

"That was Dr. Goode, JJ. She'd like to see you in her office."

JJ gathered his books back up. He gave Mary a small smile as he stood. Mary looked up at him and silently mouthed something, but JJ couldn't make out what it was. He was a lousy lip reader.

Out in the hall, JJ unfolded the square of paper that Mary had passed to him. There was a phone number on it. Beneath the number, Mary had written, "Call me."

Now JJ understood what Mary had been silently mouthing.

"Call me."

Chapter 11

Paterson 1928

"Do you remember what you said to me when you bought this land?"

Wilhelmina Andersen was in the middle of excoriating her husband.

"Do you remember your words, Owen Andersen? Because I do!"

Wilhelmina had worked herself up to a froth.

"You said you were going to build a house on it – with your own two hands! Those were your words, Owen. 'With my own two hands!' you said. So now what are you going to do? Build a house with one hand?"

Owen sat at the kitchen table with his wife looming over him. His greatest concern was the rolling pin that she kept pounding into the palm of her left hand. Owen kept one eye on it, just in case. Meanwhile he wondered if her tirade had finally run its course, but he suspected it hadn't. Once Wilhelmina got started, there was no telling when she would stop.

"And what about work?" she said, starting up again. "You think a bottling plant needs a man with one hand?"

"Don't worry about work," said Owen. "I'm a supervisor. I'm not a line worker."

"We'll see how long that lasts," said Wilhelmina. "But for now, I want you to promise me that you'll get rid of that useless piece of land. When people get wind of what's in that lake, it won't be worth a plug nickel."

Owen said nothing.

"Come on, Owen," Wilhelmina prompted. "I want to hear you say it: 'I'm going to sell the land.'"

"I'll say no such thing," said Owen. "We're keeping the land. I'm going to finish the cabin and I'm going to get that beast."

"You! The man with one hand! You're going to chop down trees, split logs, drive nails, and slay a monster?"

"No, Billy, not me, the man with one hand," answered Owen. "Me, the man with three hands."

"So now what?" sneered Wilhelmina. "Can you no longer even count – or are you planning to grow back extra hands?"

"I'm growing back nothing," said Owen, looking his wife squarely in the eye. "And what I'm counting on is Isaac. His two hands and my one make three."

Up in his bedroom above the kitchen, Isaac knitted together the fingers of his two hands. He was praying that his parents would *please* stop arguing. Even with his door closed, he could still hear every word they said – or at least every word his mother said.

Isaac turned his head to the side. That way his mattress could muffle one ear while his pillow could muffle the other. He gazed out the window. The Andersens' house was set on a rise on the east side of town. From his bedroom, Isaac could see the moonlight gleaming on the domes and spires of Paterson. Just beyond loomed the dark black mass of Garrett Mountain, the first rise in a range of mountains that rippled and swelled from the Passaic River to the Pennsylvania border and beyond.

Somewhere out there, in one of those moonlit valleys, was Turtleback Lake. In the woods on its western shore was the foundation of an unbuilt log cabin while in the lake itself an angry turtle patrolled the depths, swimming from side to side and end to end with the handle of an ax jutting out of its back.

Chapter 12

Turtleback Lake June 2006

WHEN THE PHONE DIDN'T STOP RINGING, Deena was sure it was Judd. When she picked up the receiver, she was ready to tear his head off.

But then the voice she heard wasn't Judd's.

It was someone else – somebody she'd spoken to once before, but only once.

It was, she knew, before he could even tell her, August Andersen.

She had heard his voice only that one time on the phone – when she had made the arrangements to rent his cabin for the summer.

"I'm sorry," she said. "I thought you were someone else."

"Well, whoever that someone else is," said August, "I wouldn't want to be them."

"Oh, it's nothing, really," said Deena. "I just let myself get a little too worked up over nothing. But tell me, how are you?"

"I'm fine, thanks," said August. "And I hope what I'm about to ask won't upset you. If it does, please just say no and I'll completely understand. But what I was hoping to do was to stop by the cabin for a couple of hours to address a few maintenance issues."

There was something about August's voice that Deena found instantly soothing and calming. Moments before she had been practically throttling the receiver. Now she relaxed her grip. Then she switched the receiver to her left ear because her right ear was still a little sensitive. Judd's nibbles the afternoon before had gotten a little rough.

"I hope it's not anything that I need be concerned about?" said Deena.

"No, not at all," said August. "Just minor maintenance. But since I'm going to be in the area, I thought I should *carpe diem.*"

Carpe diem! thought Deena. *Seize the day.* Clearly she was dealing with a learned man.

"When were you thinking of coming?" asked Deena.

"This weekend, actually. I'm going to be in New York for a conference and I was hoping to shoot out there for a couple of hours on Saturday afternoon."

"That'd be fine," said Deena.

"Well, great," said August. "So figure I'll just show up, probably around one or two."

"Sure," said Deena. But she didn't want the conversation to end so quickly. She wanted to keep it going.

"I remember the last time we spoke you mentioned you were a teacher," she said. "If you don't mind my asking, what do you teach?"

"I started out in marine biology," said August. "But now I specialize in the study of fresh water bodies."

"Sounds interesting," said Deena.

"Not everybody thinks so," laughed August.

"Well, I do."

"Well, maybe then we can trade notes on Saturday," said August. "Didn't you tell me you were renting the cabin so you could work on your dissertation?"

"You've got a good memory," said Deena. "Maybe if you've got a few extra minutes you could even give it a quick look!"

What a difference a voice made! Yesterday, she was a lioness ready to decapitate Judd just for asking to take a peek. Today, she was a lamb, ready to open her books to a total stranger.

While Deena was keeping August on the line, Judd paced back and forth in front of his window. He had *tried* to call Deena – he'd found the phone number of the Andersen cabin in the Turtleback Lake directory – but the line had been busy *both* times he called. Who could she possibly be talking to for so long? So much for all of Deena's talk about wanting to remain reclusive and '*incommunicado.*'

As Judd stewed, Deena was feeling a strange exhilaration from the conversation she had just concluded. Though she was usually drawn to a certain physical type, she had always had a hankering for something completely different: a tweedy, Volvo-driving, Ivy League-ish intellectual with patches on the elbows of his herringbone jacket and tortoise shell glasses framing probing, intelligent eyes.

Deena's imagination had already turned August's voice into the embodiment of just such a man. Maybe tomorrow this elusive intellectual would finally walk into her life. But she was getting ahead of herself. She had to hold her horses. She had to remember what she was here for. Not for a man – even if he was Mr. Right. She was here for a doctor – a *Dr.* in front of her name.

Deena was reminding herself of her priorities when the phone started ringing again. Instead of dispelling the last bits of her reverie, it stirred them up again. It was probably Professor Andersen calling back with something he'd forgotten to tell her. She reached for the receiver.

"Hello," she cooed.

"Well you're a hard one to contact."

At the sound of Judd's voice, anger flooded back into Deena.

"And so?"

"So nothing," said Judd, wondering why Deena was so quick to anger. "It's just that I've been trying to call you and the phone's been busy – for quite a while."

"And?"

"And nothing," said Judd. "I was just a little surprised after what you said about wanting solitude and seclusion."

This was absolutely too much! Deena did not know Judd's little broker trick for calming down by counting backwards from ten to zero.

"Look, Judd – I don't think I have to explain to you or anyone what I'm doing on the telephone."

"Whoa!" said Judd. "I didn't mean anything. I just called because after yesterday I was just kind of hoping that maybe we could do something today – maybe go out to dinner or something."

Deena had made up her mind even before Judd was finished. Yesterday clearly had been a mistake. She wasn't going to repeat it – at least not with Judd.

"Look, Judd, I'm sorry, but yesterday was yesterday. Starting today, there'll be no more yesterdays. I've got to get back to what I came here for. I'm sorry, but that's it. Goodbye."

Then she hung up the phone.

Chapter 13

Paterson 1928

THE ONLY THING POSITIVE to be said about Owen Andersen losing his hand was this: it was his *right* hand.

For most people, this would have been bad news. But not in Owen's case. Owen was that one in ten: he was a lefty.

And Owen was the kind of man who played whatever hand life dealt him. He saw no point in bemoaning what fate had taken away. He simply set himself to the task at hand.

Now, Owen was at work on a new set of drawings.

Each night after Wilhelmina and Isaac went to bed, he sat for hours at the kitchen table – sketching, erasing and revising. He obsessed over his drawings like an engineer or an inventor. In the morning, his wife and son found no signs of how he had spent the late night hours. The plans he was drawing were out of sight, rolled up in a tube, leaning against the back wall of a closet.

The loss of his right hand did cause one particular inconvenience. Owen could no longer work the car's gearshift. So he taught Isaac how to drive.

That Isaac was only eleven didn't trouble him. The boy's legs were long enough to reach the pedals and he was tall enough to see out the windshield. Nor did Owen worry about the police. Cops were few and far between once they got out of Paterson. And once they were up in the mountains, they were even rarer.

"So now what?" snapped Wilhelmina.

She was beyond exasperation.

"First you lose your hand, and now you've lost your mind!" she said, practically screaming at her husband. "Letting Isaac drive is against the law. And it's not just your life you're risking now, you're risking his, too."

Owen hardly heard a word of what Wilhelmina was saying. In matters where he knew they would never see eye to eye, he had learned to tune her out. All Owen heard, as his wife chastised him, was the driving rain lashing against the window.

For Isaac it was different. Isaac had no choice but to go along with his dad. His mother might think that he was taking sides, but he wasn't. His parents' battles were not his. He was merely a recruit, a foot soldier, impressed into service.

"Don't worry," Isaac told his mom when his father was at work. "Driving's easy. There's nothing to it."

Wilhelmina could hardly believe there could be "nothing" to something that she herself had never learned how to do.

In the end, Wilhelmina's objections were simply ignored. One Friday afternoon, when Isaac arrived home from school, he saw his father waiting for him by the car in the driveway.

"Ready to roll, Isaac?" said Owen.

"I'm ready," said Isaac.

And off they went, with Isaac at the wheel and Owen calling

out lefts and rights as needed.

The last few miles they drove in the dark, on bumpy dirt roads that tunneled under overarching branches of leaf-laden limbs. Finally, Isaac pulled around one last bend and their headlights illuminated the clearing where the foundation of their cabin stood. They got out, gathered wood, made a fire, and ate. After eating, Owen pulled out the large sheet of paper that was curled up inside the cardboard tube he'd been carrying pinned between his ribcage and what was left of his right arm. He tried spreading the sheet flat on the ground, but it kept rolling back up into a tube.

"Isaac," he said. "We'll need four good size rocks to weigh down the corners. Do you think you could find some?"

Isaac knew exactly where to find rocks: down along the shoreline by the lake.

"Sure, Dad," he said. "I'll be right back."

Isaac walked down toward the lake. During the ride up, his father had tried to allay his son's fears.

"Don't worry about that turtle," he'd said. "Turtleback Lake is a big body of water. The odds of that snapper showing up in the same spot twice are next to none."

Still, Isaac was nervous. He tried to calm himself by breathing deeply and focusing on his task: finding four good-size rocks.

Isaac was cradling three large rocks in his arms and bending down to pick up a fourth when suddenly the rock he was reaching for moved! Isaac's heart skipped a beat. He dropped the three rocks in his arms and was spinning around to run away when he abruptly stopped and started to laugh. What an idiot he was being! The "rock" that had moved was a turtle – a harmless box turtle. Isaac had brought dozens of them back home to Paterson where he'd given them to friends or let them roam free in the confines of their fenced-in backyard.

Isaac picked up the rocks he'd dropped, found a fourth, and headed back to the clearing.

"Put one on each corner," said his Dad.

The woods around them were pitch black. The only light in the forest came from their campfire. Its flames hissed, snapped, and popped while casting a flickering light on the large sheet now spread out flat on the ground. The sheet was the size of an architect's blueprint and was filled with elaborate, precisely rendered diagrams and notations. They reminded Isaac of sketches he had seen by Leonardo da Vinci and Michelangelo in books at the Paterson Public Library.

Isaac looked at his father in the flickering light. He wasn't just a line supervisor in a Coca-Cola bottling plant. There was more to him.

"What is it?" asked Isaac, his eyes widening as he looked at the drawings.

"A trap," said Owen. "A trap for our little friend in the lake."

Chapter 14

Turtleback Lake June 2006

When Deena told Judd that there would be "no more yesterdays," he came crashing back to earth like Icarus. Deena hadn't just dumped him – she had destroyed him. When she had hung up the phone, Judd wanted to call her right back, but he couldn't. She'd never answer. Yet as badly as their conversation had gone, Judd was desperate to talk to her again, to fix whatever it was that had so suddenly and inexplicably gone so terribly wrong. The thought of having to wait until their paths crossed by chance was unbearable.

For twenty-four hours, Judd agonized over what to do. The plan he finally came up with bordered on the insane, but Judd wasn't in his right mind. He was a man spurned; he was capable of doing practically anything.

Judd walked back and forth on his deck. He'd been pacing out there for almost an hour. His fingers were crossed, like a kid making a wish. Earlier, he had actually knelt down and prayed to

God that Deena would stick to her routine. At 1:25, his wishes and prayers were answered. Across the lake, a tiny figure walked down to the water. Judd raised his binoculars and adjusted the focus.

When Deena reached the edge of the lake, she stopped. The white terry cloth robe she was wearing slipped from her shoulders and fell to the ground. For a moment she just stood there, sleek and statuesque in her black one-piece. Judd's heart raced. He waited until she was in the lake, face down in the water, swimming out toward the dock. Then he raced down the wooden steps that zigzagged from his deck to his dock. He took the steps two at a time. His bathing suit was already on. As he raced the length of the long dock, Judd kicked off his topsiders and tossed aside the pink polo shirt he'd been wearing. Then, without breaking his stride, he plunged off the end of the dock into the lake.

Judd had never in his life swum as far as he was about to. But he was a man in love, and there was no stopping him.

* * *

Deena sat bolt upright.

She'd been in the middle of a dream when suddenly the dock beneath her began to rock. Deena looked around frantically.

Suddenly, from out of nowhere, Judd Clayton's head popped up, dripping wet. He hauled himself halfway out of the water and rested with his forearms at the edge of the dock.

"Jesus Christ, Judd!" cried Deena. "You just scared the daylights out of me!"

Judd tried to answer, but he couldn't. He was gasping for air.

Deena looked at him with a mixture of agitation and amazement.

"You couldn't have possibly swum here all the way from the

other side?"

Judd still couldn't speak. But he could nod. *Yes, yes,* he nodded, *yes he had.*

"Well, after the other day, I guess I should've known you were in pretty good shape," said Deena. "That's some swim."

Judd was encouraged. He had had no idea what kind of reception he was going to get.

Deena's first impulse was to stay angry at Judd. But for some reason, she couldn't. Swimming across the lake struck her as chivalrous – like a lovestruck knight trying to win a reluctant maiden's heart. It was crazy, but it was charming.

"I just had to see you," said Judd, finally catching his breath. "And not from across the lake."

As he rested on the edge of the dock, Judd's long white legs dangled in the water. Ten minutes earlier, Grundel had sensed something strange and unusual: someone was swimming out in the middle of the lake. Grundel had left his lair and risen to the surface to investigate. He patiently tracked the swimmer's progress. He followed him all the way here – to a dock floating forty or fifty yards from the lake's western shore. And now, there the man was, clinging to the dock, with his long white legs dangling languidly like khaki trousers hanging on a clothesline.

Time to bring in the laundry, thought Grundel.

He banked in the water and went in for the attack. But suddenly, the languidly dangling legs were gone.

* * *

"Can I come up?" Judd had asked.

Deena had hesitated.

Was letting Judd up on the dock any different from letting him into her cabin? She sighed. What was she thinking? The dock was out in the middle of the lake. What had happened inside the cabin could never happen out here – in the middle of the lake in broad daylight.

"Sure, why not?" said Deena. "Come on up."

Judd pushed down with his arms and lifted himself straight out of the water. He was barely erect when something thudded against the side of the dock. The dock lurched and Judd's feet went sliding out from beneath him. He fell backwards into the lake with his arms flailing.

Deena peered over the edge of the dock. Judd had vanished.

"Judd?" she called. "Where are you? Judd!"

Suddenly Judd popped back up to the surface, grabbed the edge of the dock, and scrambled back up. He had no idea how close he had come to losing a leg. Grundel's second pass, like his first, was a split second too late.

As Judd and Deena stared at the water, they heard a harsh scraping sound coming from beneath the dock. The dock rocked. Deena reached for Judd. He wrapped her in his arms.

"What's going on?" she asked.

"I don't know," said Judd. "But don't worry. You're safe. I'm here."

They waited, watching the water, but nothing else happened. Whatever had rammed the dock seemed to have gone. But Deena was still unnerved. She made no effort to remove Judd's arms. She let her head rest against his chest. She could hear and feel his heart. It was beating fast. Pressed closely against him, Deena could feel where some of that blood was rushing.

"I've got something I want to tell you," said Judd.

"Tell me later," said Deena.

For the moment, she didn't want to talk. For the moment,

she just wanted to feel safe and protected, with the arms of a man wrapped around her.

Chapter 15

Turtleback Lake October 2006

"Take a knee everybody," said Coach Lupo.

It was the middle of practice, but Bill knew he had to address the Ian Copeland issue. What had happened to Ian had to be turned into something positive. It had to be turned into a rallying cry for the team, something to bind the Snappers even closer together.

Standing in the long slanting rays of the late afternoon sun, Coach Lupo flashed back to an old black-and-white movie. He heard the voice of Knute Rockne – or was it Vince Lombardi? – addressing his team. Coach Lupo tried to channel that voice.

"Men," he began. "What happened to Ian Copeland didn't just happen to him. There are eighty of us out here on this field. But in football, eighty doesn't count. In football, eighty equals one. We are all one. And when any one of us gets hurt, we all feel it."

Coach Lupo paused to let the gravity of his words sink in.

"When we go out on the field this Saturday," he continued, "Ian Copeland is going out there with us. He'll be here," – Coach Lupo pounded his fist against his chest – "and he'll be here."

Coach Lupo tapped the side of his head with his index finger.

"George!" he called.

"Yes, Bill," said Coach Jenkins, straightening himself up from a slouch.

"Hand these out."

Coach Lupo gave Coach Jenkins a handful of decals. A local print shop had run them off for him. They were the crack-and-peel kind.

JJ looked at the sticker. It was a foot with speed lines swooshing from the heel as if the foot was swinging forward like a kicker's. There was a number on the foot. Number 13. Ian had always laughed when JJ suggested that thirteen was unlucky, and after all his game-winning kicks, JJ had come to agree with him. Now he wasn't so sure.

The players peeled off the backs of the decals and stuck the stickers on the sides of their helmets. JJ slapped his right in front.

"Now remember, boys," said Coach Lupo, hoping for a strong finish. "Whenever you make a tackle, or catch a pass, or block a kick, you're not doing it alone. Ian Copeland is there – doing it with you!"

Just as he had hoped, the players sensed his speech was over. They stood and roared, while squeezing their heads back into their helmets.

* * *

When practice was over, JJ lingered in the showers until he thought everyone else was gone. He was in no hurry to leave. It was going to be a long bike ride home without Ian at his side, pushing him to go faster.

JJ was sitting on a bench in the deserted locker room, bent over his sneakers, tying his laces when the toe of a sneaker entered his field of vision. He looked up.

"Here," said Bobby Savarese, thrusting a wooden box at JJ. "This is for you."

JJ looked at the box.

"Open it," said Savarese.

JJ fingered aside the small metal clasp that held the lid shut. Inside was the shell of the snapper JJ had killed at Ted Tanner's Pet and Turtle Shop. Now it was shiny and hardened with a baked enamel finish.

Savarese reached down and knocked on the shell with his knuckles.

"Come with me," he said.

JJ finished tying his sneaker and followed Savarese out to the parking lot. Savarese's souped-up red Chevy was the only car still there.

"Give me the cup," he said.

JJ reached into the box and removed the enameled shell. For a moment JJ thought back to the turtle soup he had eaten the night of the freshman team dinner. JJ didn't like snappers, but what had this one ever done to him to deserve what he had done to it?

Savarese took the cup from JJ. He walked to the back of his car, crouched down, and chocked the shell beneath the tire of his rear wheel.

"Watch this," he said to JJ, climbing into the front seat.

Savarese gunned the engine. Four hundred plus horsepower roared. Then he shifted the car into reverse and rolled back three feet. He looked out the driver's side window at JJ.

"Check it out," he ordered.

JJ bent down and picked up the snapper's shell. A three-thousand pound Chevy had rolled right over it and it wasn't even cracked.

"It'll do," said Savarese.

"I guess it will," said JJ.

"Wanna ride home?" Savarese asked him.

"No thanks," said JJ. "I've got my bike."

Chapter 16

Turtleback Lake June 2006

"Dad!"

JJ had come home earlier than usual that afternoon. He didn't know whether his father was home, so he called for him as he came through the front door. When there was no answer, JJ went out onto the deck. Maybe his dad would be there. But he wasn't. It was a little strange, because his father's car was parked in the driveway out front.

JJ leaned against the railing. It was a beautiful June day. The sun was high, hot and yellow and puffy white clouds dotted the cerulean sky.

JJ looked across the water. Something in the distance caught his eye. There were two people on a floating dock over near the far shore.

JJ's father had left a pair of binoculars out on the railing. JJ reached over and raised them to his eyes. He hardly could believe what he saw when he focused on the two figures on the dock. It was his father – with his arms around a woman in a black bathing suit.

JJ put the binoculars back down on the railing. He felt like a kid who'd just walked in on his parents at the wrong time. It was awkward.

But even with binoculars, JJ would've missed what happened next between his father and the woman on the dock.

They were having a conversation.

"So," said Deena. "You said you wanted to tell me something earlier. What was it?"

"I know about an opening here in town," said Judd.

"What do you mean – *an opening?*" asked Deena.

"The high school principal just retired," said Judd. "An unexpected health problem. The town needs to fill the spot before September."

"And?" said Deena, looking at Judd closely.

"Well," said Judd. "It's just that the other day you said what you really wanted was to become a principal. Maybe this could be your chance."

Judd paused. This was the big plan he had swum across the lake to deliver.

"I know a lot of people here in town," he said. "People on the school board, on the town council. I think I could give you a real leg up."

"A leg up," said Deena. "I like the sound of that."

Then she lifted up her right leg, swung it over Judd and rolled on top of him.

Chapter 17

Turtleback Lake 1928

FOR SEVERAL WEEKS, Isaac and his dad did no work on the cabin. All they worked on was the trap.

As it began to take shape, Isaac saw it was more than just a trap – it was a kind of cage made of laths woven into a tight mesh of two-inch squares. Owen and Isaac wrapped wire around each and every lath and joint.

"What's the wire for, Dad?" asked Isaac.

"Reinforcement," said Owen. "That snapper would chew right through wood. In fact, I think we should triple wrap the whole thing, okay Isaac?"

"Whatever you say," said Isaac.

When the cage was finally finished, it was six feet across the front, eight feet front to back and five feet high. On one side was a trap door that slid up and down in a greased, lubricated track. The trap door was held open by a catch that was triggered by a lever inside the cage. On the bottom, four six-foot lengths of steel cable were attached, one to each corner. At the end of each cable was a sack made of steel mesh.

On top of the cage, about a foot from the rear, was a small square opening.

"What's the hole for?" asked Isaac.

"To drop in the bait," said his dad.

After they completed the trap, Isaac and his dad set to work building a large wooded platform to go on top of it. A square was cut out to align with the bait hole.

One night as they sat around their kitchen table in Paterson, Wilhelmina asked for a progress report.

"So when is this cabin going to be finished?"

Wilhelmina was getting impatient. How many more weekends was she expected to spend alone in Paterson?

"It's coming along nicely," said Owen. "Wouldn't you say, Isaac?"

Isaac looked down at his plate.

"Well, Isaac," said his mother. "Is it – or is it not – coming along nicely?"

"It's coming along, mom," said Isaac. "But Rome wasn't built in a day."

Isaac often used the same clichés his parents used when they were talking to him.

"Who's talking about Rome?" said Wilhelmina. "I'm not talking about the Coliseum, Isaac, I'm talking about a little cabin in the woods."

"Don't pester the boy," Owen said to his wife. "You'll be seeing that cabin soon enough. It'll be worth the wait."

Wilhelmina shook her head. Why was it so difficult to get information from these two?

* * *

The sun had gone down but the surface of the lake was still shimmering with light. A huge white moon was rising in the east. It looked low enough to reach out and touch.

But Owen Andersen knew the moon would not stay so big or so low for long. Like a helium balloon, it would soon float high into the sky, still round and white, but reduced to the size of a quarter. Still, the bright, moonlit night was perfect for their purpose.

As the moon rose, it seemed to be looking down, squinting its eyes to see what the boy and man were doing. The moon had never seen such a strange and cumbersome craft plying the waters of Turtleback Lake at night.

In the distance, Turtleback Rock glowed a ghostly white. To Owen Andersen, the rock looked like the crown of a great giant's skull. He imagined the rest of its enormous white skeleton standing upright underwater, reaching all the way down to the bottom of the fathomless lake. As Owen and Isaac struggled to row their awkward craft, the distant rock grew slowly closer. Then, about a half-mile from shore, something suddenly occurred to Isaac.

Isaac glanced desperately around the platform. All he saw were four wire-mesh bags, each one full of boulders, attached to steel cables.

"Dad!" he cried. "We've got to go back!"

"What are you talking about, Isaac," said Owen. "Why?"

"We've forgotten the bait!" said Isaac.

Owen chuckled.

It was strange, but during all the time that Owen and Isaac had spent building the trap, during all their car rides back and forth, Owen had never once mentioned what they were going to use for bait. Isaac had imagined many possibilities: a rabbit, perhaps, or maybe a large chunk of meat. But for some reason, in the end, Isaac had ultimately decided that his father would use a lamb's head purchased from their butcher in Paterson.

But now, looking around the deck of their moonlit raft, Isaac saw nothing: no meat, no rabbit, no lamb's head.

"Don't worry, Isaac," said Owen. "I've got the bait."

"Where?" said Isaac. "I don't see anything."

For a moment, Owen let go of the oar he'd been rowing with the one hand he had left.

"It's right here," he said, patting himself on the leg.

Chapter 18

Turtleback Lake October 2006

THE REAL ESTATE MARKET in Turtleback Lake was dead and the reason was no longer a matter for debate. And the cause of the problem was only getting worse.

First, there'd been the increased number of "little nips" during the summer. Then came Joanne Sully's toe. Then came Ian Copeland's right foot. Even Judd would agree that changing the name of the high school football team would do little to improve things now.

Judd felt helpless. There was nothing he could do for his clients. Former prospects openly scoffed when he tried to lure them back with drastically reduced prices. One woman, appalled by what she perceived as Judd's gross insensitivity, practically bit his head off.

"Please don't talk to me about lower prices!" she snapped, "when the real price could be an arm and a leg – either mine or my children's. Please – do not call again!"

The woman slammed down the receiver. Judd was getting used to it.

In the scheme of things, Judd knew his problem was relatively minor. So he'd lose some commissions. So his income would be down this year. At the same time, he wasn't in a physical therapy facility learning to walk with a prosthetic limb, like Ian Copeland. And he wasn't being hounded day and night – like Chief Rudolph – by townspeople who were demanding he "get that snapper." Even Coach Lupo had a new set of problems to contend with. Without Ian Copeland's right leg booting field goals and extra points, the Snappers had narrowly eked out victories the last two weeks.

And then there was JJ.

How could JJ not be scarred by what had happened to him and Ian that night? Of the two boys, he'd gotten off easier, but still – what a nightmare to live through. And then there was the guilt. It had been JJ's idea to go swimming that night. Ian had said he didn't want to. JJ could still hear Ian's voice in his head: "It's late and I've got a ton of homework." Yet JJ had urged him. "C'mon," he'd said. "Just a quick dip!"

You could say all you want, but there it was – the bottom line. If it hadn't been for JJ, Ian would still have two feet.

"And if it hadn't been for you," said Judd, "Ian would've bled to death that night. You dragged him back onto the dock. You called 9-1-1. You saved his life."

But it was hard for JJ to see things that way. And at some level, Judd understood.

The situation in Turtleback Lake was bleak and only one thing was going to improve it: whatever was lurking in Turtleback Lake had to be found, captured, and killed.

When Judd walked into Bonds' he saw Chief Rudolph having

coffee at the counter.

"Mind if I join you?" he asked.

"It's a free country," said Chief Rudolph.

Judd sat down on a stool and ordered a cup of coffee.

"Look," said Chief Rudolph, as if they were already in the middle of a conversation. "It's not as if snapping turtles haven't always been in the lake. For God's sake, Judd, there are snappers in every lake up here."

Chief Rudolph emptied his cup with a quick gulp so the waitress could refill it.

"Think about the Jersey shore, Judd. Millions of people go there. You think there aren't sharks swimming in those waters? You think rip tides don't sweep people out to sea? You think people don't break their necks in the surf? For chrissakes, Judd, a few snapping turtles is nothing in comparison!"

"Nothing till now," said Judd. "A little nip is one thing. A foot is another. Whatever's in our lake has got to be one *helluva* whopper."

"Well, it didn't get to be a whopper overnight," said Chief Rudolph. "It's had to have been out there for God only knows how long. Who can even begin to guess how long this thing's been around?"

"I can," said a voice from behind them.

Chief Rudolph and Judd swiveled around. A tall slender man in tortoise shell glasses was standing behind them. Apparently he had slipped into Bonds' during their conversation. For the past minute, he'd been eavesdropping.

"Jesus Christ, Andersen!" said Chief Rudolph. "You practically gave me a heart attack sneaking up behind us like that."

"Sorry," said August.

"Forget about sorry," said Chief Rudolph. "Just tell me what you meant by 'I can.'"

Chapter 19

Turtleback Lake 1958

"THE MOON WAS FULL THAT NIGHT," began Owen Andersen.

He was starting to tell a story to his grandson, August.

August was five and he had just asked a question that had been on his mind since before he could even speak.

"What happened to your leg, Grandpa?"

Owen Andersen's right leg ended just below the knee. From there on down he wore a wooden peg leg just like a pirate's. Owen was also missing his right hand. August wondered about that, too, but that's not what he'd asked about. He had asked, "What happened to your leg, Grandpa."

And Owen had begun to tell him.

"The moon was full that night. I'd like to tell you it was an August moon, August, but it wasn't. It was a September moon, and it was the biggest, fullest moon I'd ever seen. The moon looked like it had come down close to earth just to get a better look at two people – your father and me. We were out in the middle of the lake on the strangest looking vessel you ever did see. It was a craft that your father and I had built and it really wasn't a boat at all. It was a kind of wooden raft set on top of a cage we had built out of wire and wood. And we were out there that night to have our revenge on a horrible monster."

August interrupted his Grandfather.

"Monsters aren't real, Grandpa," he said. "They're only in books and movies."

"There you're wrong, my boy," said Owen. "I don't mean to scare you, Augie boy, but monsters are real, very real. And some of them are out to get us. That's just the way it is, August, so you might as well get used to the idea. It's good versus evil out there, us versus them. And in this case, your father and I were up against a giant snapping turtle."

"How did you know he was out there?" asked August.

"I'd seen him, Augie," said Owen. "I'd even fed him once."

Grandpa raised his right arm, the one that ended before his wrist. "He'd already eaten my right hand."

Augie eyed the stump at the end of his grandpa's right arm.

"People talk about phantom limbs, August. They talk about getting itches or pain in hands or legs they no longer have."

Augie imagined trying to scratch an itch on a hand that was no longer there. It was a strange thing to think.

"For me, Augie, it was different. My missing hand didn't hurt or itch. In my case, I felt the bones of my missing hand trying to claw their way out of the turtle's belly. Part of me – my hand – was a prisoner inside that beast. But no matter how much my hand clawed and scratched, it wasn't getting out. It was trapped. There was only one way for my hand to escape. The beast had to be killed – and I had to do it. And that is what your Daddy and I were doing out on the lake that moonlit night."

Grandpa Owen shifted his grandson from one thigh to the other. When the boy was comfortably settled, he continued.

"We paddled out to the middle of the lake. Then we lifted the trap door of the cage and we waited."

"Waited for what, Grandpa?"

"We waited for the beast to come and take the bait."

"What did you use for bait, Grandpa?"

The boy's brain was teeming with possibilities.

"I used what I knew it liked. I used one of my limbs. I greased my right leg with animal fat so that I could slip it in and out quickly without getting snagged. Then I slid it into the hole we had made in the top of the trap, and we waited."

"How did you know he would come, Grandpa?"

"I didn't know. But I had a *feeling*. The moon had been full the first time he attacked. I thought maybe the full moon might draw him out again. I did mention there was a full moon that night, didn't I, Augie?"

"Yes, Grandpa, you did, several times. A September moon."

"Yes, well, so as I was saying, we sat there and waited. And as we waited, I began to feel certain the turtle was coming. 'He's coming,' I said to your Daddy. And your Daddy said, 'How do you know?' And I said, 'I can feel my hand drawing near.'

"The lake shimmered in the moonlight. The surface was still, calm, flat and shiny. Then suddenly your Daddy cried out, 'Look!' Your Daddy pointed. And I saw what he was pointing at. Cutting through the water like the fin of a shark was a wooden handle – the handle of the ax I had planted in the beast's back the night it had attacked us.

"'Get ready!' I told your Daddy."

"Get ready for what?" asked August. "What was my Daddy

supposed to do?"

"After the turtle went for my leg and the trap door dropped, your Daddy's job was to cut the rope that secured the cage to our raft and then shove the boulders in the steel mesh sacks over the side."

"What would that do?" asked Augie.

"Remember, the steel mesh bags full of boulders were connected by cables to the bottom of the trap. The plan was for those heavy rocks to drag the cage and the turtle in it to the bottom of the lake. We were going to bury him in the deep dark depths from which he came."

"So what happened. Grandpa?"

"At first, only a few inches of the ax handle protruded above the surface. But as the monster approached, it stuck out higher and higher. It was closing fast. I wiggled the toes of my right foot to make our bait seem lively. Then, like a car crashing into a wall, the turtle struck. As it entered the cage, the handle of the ax was knocked backwards from its upright position. The trap door dropped down and the turtle began thrashing furiously. Through the hole in the top of the trap, it eyed us with unspeakable hatred. You've heard the saying, *'If looks could kill?'* Well, if they could, none of us would be here today. Your Daddy and I would be dead, and you, my boy, would never have been born. But the monster's eyes, yellow and horrible as they were, had no power to harm us. The beast's weapons were its claws, its jaw, and its razor sharp beak. Its eyes? I spat in them! Then I told your Daddy, 'Cut the rope!' Your Daddy sawed through the rope. 'Now shove the boulders overboard!' I told him. 'It's time to bury this bad boy!'"

"But what about your leg, Grandpa? Did he bite it off when it was inside the trap?"

"No, August. I pulled my leg out of the trap in the nick of time.

That's what frustrated the turtle so much. If he was going to die, he at least wanted to take one of us with him."

"But then what happened to your leg, Grandpa?"

"Your Daddy had pushed the boulders to the edge of the platform. Ten seconds more and that turtle would be gone forever. But then, I did myself in. You remember how I told you I'd covered my leg with grease so I could pull it out quickly when the turtle struck? Well, I slipped on that damn grease. It was like slipping on a bar of soap in the tub. My luck was bad. My foot slipped right back into the hole I'd just pulled it out of. It all happened at once. Your father pushed the boulders off, I slipped, the turtle snapped. We sent him to his grave, but he had one last supper on his way."

"How come you didn't bleed to death, Grandpa?"

"I would have, August, if it wasn't for your father. I went into shock. It was days before I was aware of anything. I was in a hospital bed, still dopey from morphine. I only know what happened from what your Daddy told me later."

Owen Andersen nodded toward his son.

"Go ahead, Isaac," he said. "Tell Augie what happened next."

"I pulled Grandpa up onto the platform. Then I ripped off my shirt and tore it into long strips, which I used to make a tourniquet. I tried to row the platform back to shore, but the oarlocks were too far apart for one boy. I couldn't do it. So I climbed into the water and dragged Grandpa with me. I put an arm across his chest and side-stroked all the way back to shore. I don't know how I made it, but I did. Then I dragged Grandpa to the car and laid him across the backseat. I sped off in search of the nearest hospital I could find. I was driving so fast, a policeman pulled me over. Before he could even start in about me driving, he saw Grandpa in the backseat. 'What's happened to him?' he asked. 'Lost his leg,' I said. Then the two of us lifted Grandpa into the backseat of the police car. He put on his siren and flashers and we sped off even faster than I'd been driving."

"So you and Grandpa killed the turtle?" August asked his father.

Isaac Andersen nodded.

"We sent him to his grave."

But for the rest of Grandpa Owen's life, from the night he lost his foot till the day he finally died, he was plagued by doubt. He and Isaac had sent the beast to the bottom of the lake, of that he was sure. Yet he never felt that his own lost limbs were fully at rest. He had a troubling sense that they were in motion – sometimes far away, sometimes near, sometimes down deep, sometimes rising toward the surface.

Chapter 20

Turtleback Lake October 2006

THOSE WHO PAINT on private or public property may think their graffiti is art – a form of creative expression to which they are somehow entitled. Yet I'd like to see these same "artists" should they someday become property owners themselves. Then let us hear how they feel when their property has served as the canvas for someone else's creative expression. Let's hear then what they have to say about 'creative freedom.' I think the song they would sing then would be very much in harmony with the one being sung in this column today.

So began the editorial Marc Bozian was working on for Thursday's *Turtleback Gazette*. Marc already had written an account of the incident for the paper's front page. This editorial, Marc's first op-ed piece, was a chance to spread his journalistic wings and fly beyond the constraints of who, what, when, where, and why.

Marc was articulating a rage he felt sure every resident of Turtleback Lake shared. As Marc wrote, he felt that he was speaking for the people.

For time immemorial, long before even the first braves of the noble Lenape Indians hunted in these woods and fished these waters – our lake has been distinguished by a single distinctive landmark: The white isle of rock that gives our lake and community their names. The Lenape, legend tells us, considered this rock to be sacred – the shell of a great white turtle that carried the lake and all its riches on its back into these mountains. The boldest Lenape brave would not have dared to paddle his canoe within a hundred feet of this sacred stone. To stain its sacred surface with dyes of colored berries would have been an unthinkable sacrilege.

And throughout the centuries since the red man has departed, this rock had remained a hallowed symbol of our community. No one has ever dared to deface its pure white surface. No one, that is, until this Monday night, when someone – or some ones – wrapped in the black cloak of night, defaced our town's most precious landmark with a galling cartoon of our high school football team's Snapper emblem.

We have always been proud of our young people's athletic achievements. This defacement, this defilement, this disgusting display of degradation, however, is a harsh wakeup call – especially in light of the horrible occurrences that have taken place in recent weeks.

It is the duty of all of us who hold true to the values of this community to help root out not only the monster that lives in the depths of our lake, but also any monsters that lurk within us.

Marc read over what he had written in long hand. A few words would have to be edited, maybe a few more alliterations added, but otherwise, Marc was pleased – *perfectly pleased.*

Marc set his notepad alongside his keyboard and began typing. When he was done, he gazed out of his cluttered cubicle at the claustrophobic chaos of *The Turtleback Gazette's* office. Though his eyes were open, Marc saw nothing. He was looking inward for the perfect title. Then it came to him.

He typed it – in capitals. Then he tried highlighting and bold-facing the letters. Then he increased the point size. There. Maybe it wasn't perfect. But it was good:

SHELL SHOCKED!

Who in Turtleback Lake wouldn't read that?

Deena Goode stood on the stage in front of a packed auditorium. She had stood waiting patiently as students filed in and found their seats. Dozens of conversations were still going on, but she would extinguish them like little fires, simply by beginning to speak.

"As a student body," she began, "we have suffered a great loss."

Nobody in the audience stopped talking.

Deena looked irritably at the microphone. She turned it from side to side in her hand. She loathed audio-visual equipment. Something always malfunctioned. But this time, at least, the fix was easy. The microphone was simply off. All she had to do was turn it on. She found the switch, gave it a flick, and started again.

"As a student body," she repeated, "we have suffered a great loss."

Deena paused to allow any lingering conversations to end.

"What happened to Ian Copeland is something he will have

to live with for the rest of his life. And the rest of us – his friends, classmates, teammates, and teachers – will never forget. When Ian returns, I expect all of us to show him the same kind of understanding and compassion we would hope for if we were in his shoes."

Looking into the crowd, Deena noticed that a number of students in the first few rows were wincing.

She thought for a moment and then it hit her. *Shoes! Plural. Dammit!*

What was she thinking? Ian Copeland wouldn't be wearing *shoes* – he'd be wearing *a shoe*, singular. She cursed herself for not preparing something in advance. Extemporaneous speaking was a landmine. But what could she do now? She plowed ahead before any wiseacre could seize on her *faux pas*.

"But Ian's loss is no excuse for the actions of those who defiled Turtleback Rock last night. Some people might say that what they did was simply 'acting out.' But I disagree. I say acting out is no excuse! I say it is adding insult to injury.

"So I stand here today to ask you, in fact to deputize you, to help find the perpetrators of this shameful deed. If you know something, say something. If you are afraid of retaliation, if you think that telling on someone is "squealing," I ask you to think again. Do not be cowed into silence by those who would have you be their mute accomplices. If it makes you feel better, report what you know anonymously. But do not remain silent. Do not allow yourself to be intimidated."

Deena now had everyone's undivided attention. She paused for dramatic effect then continued with her grand finale.

"And I'll conclude by saying this: I believe whoever committed this shameful act sits among us today. Look to your right and look to your left, look at the person sitting in front of you and look at the person behind you."

Deena paused again. As instructed, the students in the auditorium looked awkwardly about.

"One of you," said Deena, her voice now rising like a courtroom lawyer's, "has just looked into the eyes of the vandal who has shamed this community. Let him or her or them come forth on their own – or I assure you they will be brought forth by others."

Dr. Goode dismissed the students back to their classrooms. She turned off the microphone and secretly congratulated herself for the "him, her or them" at the end of her speech. It had been spontaneous but spot on. By adding that "her," no one could accuse her of being sexist, though she'd be willing to bet her life that the perpetrator wasn't female.

Oscar Hall was on his way back to the boiler room after replacing a bank of lights that had blown in the school's faraway E-wing. As unobtrusively as possible, he tried to navigate through the congestion of young people that crowded the hallways between classes.

Oscar limped along like a maimed and aging member of an otherwise strong and healthy herd. It had been ages since he'd been as young and strong as the students around him. But having dragged his bum leg through these halls for decades, he knew their youth for what it was: Fleeting. The most precious thing they'd ever possess was even now slipping through their grasp. In a flash, their youth, their beauty, and even their dreams would be behind them. And they didn't even know it.

Oscar tried to go about his business as invisibly as possible but there was always someone – invariably a boy – who would use his infirmity to get a laugh. How many times had Oscar walked down these tiled halls and heard laughter welling up behind him? And he knew what was happening without turning around. Someone was aping him. But of course, they were not content to simply mimic him. They had to exaggerate his limp for comic effect.

Oscar no longer turned around because once, years ago, he had.

He remembered it like it was yesterday. He had replayed the scene in his mind a million times, like it was roll of game film he was studying.

Oscar had turned suddenly and grabbed the boy by the collar. Then he had lifted the boy off the ground. It was funny how the kid had tried to run away even though his two feet were a foot above the floor. At that point, the laughter had stopped pretty quickly. Oscar had had an urge to slam the boy against the metal lockers that lined the corridor, but he had resisted the temptation. It was a good thing. Even back then, assaulting a student, regardless of the provocation, would get a man fired. And Oscar had needed the job. He needed it still. So Oscar had simply dropped the kid to the floor. He could still remember the sudden stink that told him the boy had crapped his pants.

So as he had done a thousand times, Oscar ignored the titters and giggles he heard behind him. Even as the laughter grew to hysteria, he ignored it.

Then suddenly the laughter stopped.

Ken Lubowsky couldn't understand why. He was in the middle of getting the biggest laugh he'd ever gotten. What Ken couldn't see, however – because his view was blocked by Oscar's back – was that Coach Lupo had just rounded a corner and was walking straight down the hall toward them.

"Hello, Oscar," he called.

"Hi, Bill."

Hearing Coach Lupo's voice, Ken turned sideways like someone trying to hide behind a tree.

Coach Lupo scanned the crowd of onlookers. Not one of them dared to meet his gaze. They all stared down at their feet. Lupo summarily dismissed them all in his mind: a ball-less bunch of cowards, followers and losers.

"Lubowsky," he said, "I'd like to have a word with you – now – in my office."

Then Lupo turned and walked back down the hallway with Oscar Hall limping at his side.

Chapter 21

Turtleback Lake 1965

LIKE ALL KIDS, August Andersen loved summers: almost three full months without school. But his summers were even better than most other kids' because he spent his in paradise. From late June till early September, August spent every single day swimming, fishing and exploring Turtleback Lake.

Isaac Andersen tried not to give his son the fears that he himself harbored within. Why make the boy unnecessarily nervous? After all, it had been over thirty years since he and his father had sent the great snapper to its grave. To his knowledge, in all those years, there had never been another incident.

Still, Isaac felt a nagging uneasiness, especially when Grandpa Owen visited the cabin.

"I don't know what it is, Isaac," Grandpa Owen would say looking out toward the lake. "But whenever I'm here, I still get that feeling deep in my gut – like my bones are still moving around out there."

"Well, for goodness sakes, Dad, just don't mention it to Augie," said Isaac. "The last thing I want is for him to develop some kind of turtle complex."

Augie had heard his grandfather tell the tale of the Great Snapping Turtle so many times it had lost all its terror. It was like *The Wizard of Oz*. The first time he'd seen the movie, he'd been terrified by the flying monkeys. By the tenth time, he was eagerly pointing out the fine wires that lifted the monkeys off the ground.

Still, when it came to the lake, Isaac had three hard-and-fast rules for his son.

"*Number one*: never swim out past the floating dock. *Number two*: never swim at night. And *number three*: never, ever go swimming when the moon is full."

"All right, Dad, I hear you," said Augie. "You've told me that a million times."

By age twelve, Augie swam like a fish. And though he'd never gone swimming after dark or when the moon was full, he had slowly and over time stretched the boundaries of how far out he swam. Often Isaac would look out from the cabin and see Augie and a friend splashing in the water far beyond the floating dock.

Then Isaac would take a deep breath and remind himself that there was nothing to worry about. His fears were baseless. He had to just let go and – how did his mother used to put it? – let God.

The ultimate test came the day he and Augie were sitting in the hot summer sun with their legs dangling over the side of the floating dock.

"You know what I'd really like to try?" said Augie.

"No," said his father. "What?"

"I'd like to try skin diving."

It was as if Isaac had just taken a harpoon through his heart.

This was the last thing he wanted Augie to do. And he blamed it all on that damn TV show – *Sea Hunt* – with Lloyd Bridges. The show made skin diving look so adventurous. And every afternoon Augie was glued to the tube watching reruns of it.

"I don't know, Augie," said Isaac. "Skin diving is an expensive hobby. And it's dangerous."

"Ah, c'mon, Dad," said Augie. "I'll pay for the equipment. And I'll learn how to dive properly. I'll take lessons. And I'll pay for them, too."

"You'll pay?" said his dad. "Well, I suppose if you can pay, you can do it."

Isaac thought he was buying himself time – years of it. Augie's allowance was just fifty cents a week. It would take him forever to save enough money to pay for skin diving equipment and lessons.

But Isaac was wrong.

The next afternoon Augie burst into the cabin with an announcement.

"I got a job!" he said.

"Where?" asked Isaac. "Doing what?"

"At Bonds," said Augie. "Doing whatever – clearing tables, doing dishes, sweeping up. Mr. Bonds says he'll pay me a dollar fifty an hour – under the table."

Isaac could hardly believe his ears. Then things got even worse.

"And look at this," said Augie.

He handed his father a rolled up copy of *The Turtleback Gazette*. The paper was folded open to the classified page. A small ad had been enthusiastically circled.

Isaac read the ad.

Somebody was selling his kid's old skin diving equipment cheap.

"I already called the guy," said Augie. "And he said I could pay in installments. Isn't that great, Dad?"

"Yeah," said his father. "It's great – really great."

Chapter 22

Turtleback Lake June 2006

DEENA WAS CHECKING THE BRIE on the counter to see if it had begun to soften when she heard the sound of gravel crunching in the drive.

"Oh my God!" she said. "He's here."

Her heart began to race. It was ridiculous, but she couldn't help it. Ever since they'd spoken on the phone, Deena had built up a vivid fantasy around August. All morning she'd been a wreck. Now it was Saturday afternoon, and he was here. She knew she should just calm down. He was probably going to turn out to be some pudgy bald-headed guy with bad teeth.

Still, before peeking out the window, Deena went to the mirror and fixed her hair one last time. Then she looked out.

"Oh my God!" she said.

Her fantasy had fallen short – *way* short.

August was tall – at least six one or two; his hair was a shade of blonde that most people have to dye for; and his face, from his pale green eyes to the cleft in his chin, was movie-star handsome. Deena suddenly panicked. August was *too* good, *too* handsome. He was out of her league. But what could she do?

Deena opened the door and, affecting a nonchalance that she didn't in the least feel, she leaned against the doorframe.

"Dr. Andersen, I presume?" she said.

"Just plain August will do," he answered. "And you, I presume, are my tenant – Deena Goode?"

"In the flesh," said Deena, reaching out to shake August's hand.

"Have you been enjoying the cabin?" he asked.

"More than I can say," said Deena. "It's been wonderful."

"I'm so glad," said August. "As I said on the phone, there are just a couple of things I want to attend to as long as I'm in the area. I don't think they should take very long."

"Take all the time you need," said Deena. "And please, since you've come all this way, I hope you'll stay for a little bite before you leave."

"A little bite sounds nice," said August. "I'll look forward to it. Thank you."

As August set to work outdoors, Deena went inside and changed into her bathing suit. She wrapped herself in her white terry cloth robe but left it untied in front. August was down on his knees examining a line that led to the septic tank when ten bare toes with brightly painted nails entered his field of vision. August's gaze scanned up Deena's bare legs and over the gentle undulations of her tight black bathing suit before reaching her eyes.

"I'm just going for a little dip," she said, smiling down at August. "If you need anything inside the cabin, help yourself. The door's open."

"Thanks," said August. "I think I should be okay."

When Deena reached the water, she let her robe slide slowly down from her shoulders. It seemed to fall to the ground in slow motion. Then, before plunging into the water, she reached up behind her head, arched back her shoulders, and slowly gathered her hair into a short ponytail. She hoped August was watching. It was the real reason she was going swimming.

After her swim, Deena toweled herself dry then changed into a pair of shorts and a short-sleeved blouse. She left the top two buttons undone.

Then she waited. It seemed hours before she heard a knock at the screen door.

"Come on in," she called.

"I'm finally finished," said August, entering the cabin. "I hope I didn't overstay my welcome."

"Don't be silly," said Deena. "Come in. I'll put something out for us to eat."

While August washed up, Deena set out bread, cheese and olives.

"Is it too early to offer you a glass of wine?" she asked when August returned from the bathroom.

"Not at all," said August. "Wine sounds great."

An hour later, the food was mostly eaten and the bottle of wine was empty. When August excused himself to use the facilities, Deena quickly uncorked a second bottle. She knew what she was doing, but she couldn't resist. She didn't want August to go yet.

When August returned to the table, his glass had been refilled.

"Tell me," said Deena, as August sat down and reached for the new glass of wine. "What first got you interested in marine biology?"

"It was when I was a kid," said August. "I spent every summer here at the lake. One summer, when I was about twelve, I took up skin diving. It changed my whole world."

"Really," said Deena. "How so?"

"It was the Sixties," said August. "Space exploration was just beginning. And for some reason, skin diving made me feel like an astronaut – floating around weightless in a strange and alien environment. After being underwater, life on dry land seemed a little dull in comparison."

"So – " said Deena. "In all your dives, what was the most interesting thing you ever found?"

"Here at the lake?" asked August.

Deena nodded.

August gazed out the window. It was dusk now. In the eastern sky, the moon was starting to rise while in the houses on the far shore lights were just beginning to come on. Deena ignored the fact that one of them was probably Judd's.

Deena noticed that August's eyes seemed glazed and faraway.

"The most interesting thing I ever found?" he said, repeating Deena's question. "It was something my father and grandfather had built long before I was even born."

"What was it?" asked Deena. "And what was it doing in the lake?"

"It was a trap – a kind of cage, really," said August. "My father and grandfather built it to catch a giant snapper. Then they sunk it to the bottom of the lake."

"And you found it?" prompted Deena.

"I did," said August. "But it wasn't quite what I expected."

"What do you mean?" asked Deena.

"What I was really looking for were the remains of the snapper – its shell and skeleton. But I didn't find them. The cage was empty. The only thing in it was an ax."

"An ax?" said Deena.

"Yes," said August, glancing over toward the fireplace. "That ax, in fact."

Deena looked at the ax that hung on two hooks above the mantelpiece.

"I have to say," said Deena with a laugh. "It did strike me as a rather odd piece of decor. I mean I could imagine someone hanging up a musket or maybe even a hockey stick – but an ax?"

"I didn't hang it for decoration," said August.

August got up and walked over to the fireplace. He reached up and ran his thumb along the edge of the blade.

"*Ouch!*" he said, pulling his hand away suddenly. "That was dumb! I cut myself."

"What were you doing?" asked Deena.

"Seeing if it was sharp enough," said August.

"Sharp enough for what?" asked Deena.

"You never know," said August. "For whatever comes up."

Chapter 23

Turtleback Lake October 2006

JUDD CLAYTON AND CHIEF RUDOLPH were both shocked to find August Andersen standing behind them at Bonds'.

For years, August had been a phantom presence in Turtleback Lake. Over the last decade, the Andersen cabin had gone largely unused, even in summertime. A few years back, Judd had run into August in the local hardware store. Though he barely knew him, Judd tried to strike up a conversation, hoping to find out if August might be interested in selling his cabin.

"Not interested," said August. "It's been in the family a long time."

"Really?" said Judd. "How long?"

"Since the Twenties," said August. "My father helped build it when he was a kid – with my grandfather."

"Well," said Judd. "If you're not interested in selling, what about renting? You rarely ever use the cabin. You could make good money with some summer rentals. I'd handle everything – tenants, payments, cleaning people."

"Thanks," said August. "But no thanks. I'm just not interested."

And that had been that – until this past summer.

August must have changed his mind because he rented the cabin on his own – without a broker. Judd kept an eye on the classified sections of all North Jersey papers and he remembered spotting an ad when he was flipping through *The Bergen Record*. Even in tiny seven-point type, the headline had popped out: *PIECE OF PARADISE.*

Of course the person who ended up renting the cabin turned out to be Deena Goode, the woman who had now thoroughly screwed up Judd's head and heart.

Judd had told himself a thousand times that he should just let go. But he couldn't. For him it hadn't been a fling. He had really liked Deena. And she had gotten under his skin – *way* under. The whole thing had been gnawing away at him for months.

And now the man who Judd suspected of screwing up everything was standing before him, telling Chief Rudolph that he thought he could guess how old the snapper in the lake might be.

"Well," said Chief Rudolph. "What's your estimate?"

"I'd say close to a hundred," said August. "Maybe more."

"Jeez, August!" burst out Chief Rudolph. "You're telling me you think this thing's been in the lake since – what? – before the First World War! That's a bit of a stretch. How do you figure?"

August looked Chief Rudolph in the eye.

"I think it's the same snapper who bit off my grandfather's arm and leg eighty years ago."

"What are you talking about?" said Chief Rudolph.

Chief Rudolph could remember August's grandfather from when he'd been a kid. He could still picture him. It was hard to forget a man who was missing both a hand and a leg.

"I always figured your Granddaddy lost his limbs working in a plant or fighting in the war. Now you're telling me a snapper did it – right here in this lake?"

"It was something my grandfather never told anybody – except me," said August. "My grandmother told him to keep his mouth shut or they'd be stuck with a worthless piece of property. Besides –"

"Besides what?" asked Chief Rudolph.

"My grandfather thought he'd taken care of the problem."

"Taken care of it? How?"

"Mind if I sit down?" asked August.

Chief Rudolph nodded at the empty stool to the left of him.

"Seat's free," he said.

August sat down. The waitress brought over a cup of coffee and poured fresh refills for Judd and the Chief.

"It all started back in the Twenties," said August. "Back when my grandfather first bought some land up here..."

At first, Judd could hardly focus on what August was saying. He kept thinking back to the summer. It was August's brief appearance back in July that had somehow put the *kibosh* on everything between him and Deena. Judd thought back with shame and anger to the night when he had looked through his telescope and spied on the two of them talking and drinking wine in Andersen's cabin. At one point, Deena had gone to the windows and lowered the blinds.

After that, Deena was never the same. She was standoffish and aloof. And by then, he had already put in a good word for her with the school board. His recommendation had definitely given her the inside track on getting the principal job at Turtleback High. And she'd gotten it. And what had he gotten in return? A big fat heartache.

At some point Judd snapped out of his funk and began listening. In spite of himself, he was riveted by August's tale. To think that a snapper who had ripped off a man's hand and leg in the 1920s could still be in the lake. It was absolutely mind-boggling.

Suddenly the door to Bonds' swung open. A lanky man in uniform, chief deputy Donald Rhodes, burst into the room.

"Hey, Chief!" he called. "You better come check out what's going on."

"What is it, Donnie? Can't you see I'm busy?"

"A bunch of guys are down at the boat basin," said the deputy. "They're going out onto the lake with gaffs and clubs and spear guns."

"What the hell do they think they're doing?" said Chief Rudolph.

"They say they're going to get the snapper themselves," said Deputy Rhodes. "They said you ain't doing –", Deputy Rhodes paused and looked around the room. There were families with children present.

Chief Rudolph rose from his stool with a groan.

"I get the message, Donny," he said. Then he turned back to Judd and August.

"You'll have to excuse me, gentlemen. But I better get down there before things get out of hand."

Chief Rudolph strode away leaving an empty stool between Judd and August.

* * *

When Chief Rudolph and Deputy Rhodes reached the town dock, an armada of rowboats, canoes, and kayaks had already set sail.

"Hey, Sully, what the hell is going on here!" called Chief Rudolph.

Jack Sully was untying the rope that tethered his red canoe to the end of the pier.

"We're tired of waiting," answered Sully. "We're taking matters into our own hands."

"I'm handling this," said Chief Rudolph.

"You're *handling* this?" said Sully, his voice full of scorn. "It's been more than a week since that kicker lost his foot, and more than three since my little girl lost her toe – and what have you done? Put up some *No Swimming* signs! With all due respect, Chief, that's like putting up *No Smoking* signs during a five-alarm fire!"

"Don't be a damn fool, Sully. Going out there in rickety little boats with sticks and stones isn't going to accomplish anything except maybe get somebody else killed or maimed. What are you going to do if this snapper attacks? Hit him with your paddle?"

"Hell, no, Chief! I'm gonna give him a lot more than a paddling."

Sully shoved his canoe away from the dock. Then he reached down and lifted up a double-barreled shotgun.

"I'm gonna blow the bloody bastard right out of its shell!"

* * *

Jack Sully loved his daughter, but his love wasn't doing her much good. There were too many other emotions dictating his actions: anger, self-pity, righteous indignation, and poor judgment. Jack also drank too much.

In the past, most of Jack's anger had been directed at his wife.

After she left him, it spread to include anyone who Jack felt was doing him an injustice. Now he was angry at the whole damn town for doing nothing about his daughter's attack.

"If it had been somebody else's child, you can be sure the lake would've been dredged," he said to anyone who sat on the bar stool next to his. "But not for *my* little girl."

If the guy on the stool next to him said, "They didn't dredge the lake after Ian Copeland's attack either," Jack would simply ignore him. His mind had no available space for counter arguments.

Now Jack Sully was out on the lake in a canoe. His daughter was home alone, wondering where he was. Usually at this hour she could find him asleep in an armchair with a beer can clutched in his hand and the TV still on. But tonight her father had never even come home.

The armada that had set out that afternoon had long since returned to port. Now, as midnight approached, Jack's canoe was the only vessel still out on the lake. Empty beer cans bobbing in the water were his only company.

When Jack had set off hours earlier, he had a full case of beer as ballast in the bottom of his canoe. Most of that ballast was now gone.

Moonlight glinted on the cans he had tossed overboard. Suddenly Jack grabbed onto the gunwales and pulled himself upright. He had to pee. As he unzipped his pants, he looked up at the round white rock glowing in the sky.

Then Jack began to croon at the moon.

"When the moon, is in someone's house, and Jupiter aligns with Mars, then peace will guide the planet, and love, love will..."

"Love will what?" he wondered. He couldn't remember.

As Jack pondered, he gazed across the water. His eyes fixed on another white rock – the one that stood out in the middle of the lake. Only now the rock wasn't white – it was yellow. Jack squeezed his eyes tightly shut, but when he reopened them, the rock was still yellow. Then he remembered – of course! The other night, somebody had given the rock a nice new coat of paint. Nobody knew who – except Jack. How could he have forgotten?

Jack's bladder was ready to burst. He looked at the empty cans floating like flotsam around his canoe. He took aim at one of them. His urine rang out against the empty can. Direct hit. *One.* Jack aimed at another. His urine resounded like rain on a tin roof. *Two.* This was fun. Maybe he could hit all twenty. That would be something. He'd have to notify Guinness – the record-keeping people, not the brewery people. Jack was now up to seven, eight.

Then, hey! What the hell was that? Something had just popped up! Jack gave it a good long squirt. Maybe he could push the damn thing back under. But he couldn't. And whatever it was, the thing didn't resound with a nice metallic ring.

Then it hit Jack.

"Holy cow!"

Jack didn't even bother to stop peeing. He just bent down to pick up his shotgun.

Standing back up, he cocked the barrels into position. Now where the hell had that damned bastard gone?

Standing in a canoe is never a good idea, especially after drinking. But Jack stood there anyway, scanning the water, his head straining from side to side.

"C'mon out, you stinking son of a bitch!" said Jack. "Show your damn face so I can blast it to kingdom come!"

Grundel had been pissed on once before. It had been a long, long time ago. He hadn't liked it then and he didn't like it now. He eyed the curved red underbelly of the canoe rocking above him.

How should he do this? Of course, ramming the canoe would

do the job quite nicely. But then another idea came to Grundel–something a bit more theatrical.

Grundel could see the man in the boat silhouetted against the moon. He was standing up, looking over the starboard side.

Grundel swam under the boat and surfaced on the port side. He reached up, first with his right claw and then with his left, and grabbed hold of the gunwale. As he pulled himself up, the canoe tipped violently. Jack Sully cursed and spun around. As he started to fall, his gun went off. For a millisecond, his eyes met Grundel's. Then Jack felt his flesh being flayed off his body as he slid across the snapper's hard, horny shell.

The cold water sobered Jack in an instant. Still, staying afloat wasn't easy while holding a shotgun in one hand. With his other hand, Jack tried grabbing the overturned canoe, but his hand kept slipping. Meanwhile, Grundel circled slowly in the depths below. He was in no rush. His prey wasn't going anywhere. Grundel looked up. There was the man, a fat man, treading water to stay afloat. Then with a powerful stroke of his webbed claws, Grundel shot upwards.

The great snapper closed his eyes and spread his jaw as wide as it would open. He struck Jack squarely between the legs with the impact of a wrecker's ball.

* * *

The phone at his bedside woke Chief Rudolph.

"Chief, sorry to wake you," said Deputy Rhodes. "But some woman just called the station. She says she was out jogging and saw a red canoe floating upside down in the lake."

"Damn fool!" muttered Chief Rudolph. "I warned him."

Now, an hour later, Rudolph and Rhodes were towing the canoe back to the town dock. Their boat was the only motorboat allowed on the lake. For years the town had rejected appeals to permit water skiing. If people wanted to jet ski or water ski, let them go to Lake Hopatcong or Lake Mohawk. But not here. Turtleback Lake was special.

When they reached the dock, Marc Bozian was waiting at the end of it.

"Any sign of a body?" he called out, before Deputy Rhodes could even secure their boat to the pier.

Chief Rudolph was in no mood for the reporter.

"Do you think we'd have left a body out there if we'd found one?" he snapped.

"Well, do you at least know whose canoe it is?"

"Sure we know," barked the Chief. "It's Jack Sully's. I watched him paddle off in it yesterday. I warned the damn fool not to go out there."

"Shouldn't you have stopped him, Chief?" said Bozian. "Surely you recognized the potential danger. Surely you had the authority to order him back to shore."

"Enough of the 'surely' crap," snapped the Chief.

The kid and his damn articles were already a stone in his shoe. Now the kid was giving him the goddamn fifth degree.

Still, Rudolph couldn't resist answering.

"Sure, I could have 'ordered' him back. Him and the fifty other men who went out with him. I had the authority. I just didn't have the manpower. Sometimes the law simply can't protect people from themselves."

"Are you suggesting that this was Jack Sully's fault?" asked Marc.

"His fault?" Chief Rudolph actually paused to reflect. "Maybe it wasn't exactly his fault. Maybe it was just his fate. What happened to him didn't have to happen, but he made damn sure that it did."

Bozian looked down. From up on the dock, he could see into the bottom of the police boat. Empty beer cans were rolling from side to side as the boat rocked.

"Where'd all the beer cans come from, Chief?"

"They were floating in the water."

"So you think alcohol was a factor?"

"It usually is, son."

Bozian looked again at the cans that had now congregated near the stern of Chief Rudolph's boat. He did a quick count. There were twenty.

"Chief, am I safe in assuming that you're looking for more than one body?" ventured Bozian.

"Why do you think?" asked the Chief.

"Surely one man didn't drink all those beers," said Marc.

"Hey – I think I told you to cut out that *'surely'* business earlier. And clearly you didn't know Jack Sully."

Jack Sully drank like a fish, thought Chief Rudolph. *And now he's with them.*

Suddenly Rudolph turned to Rhodes.

"Jeez, Donny, I completely forgot. You better get over to Sully's house and check in on his daughter. God knows what the poor kid must be thinking."

"What should I tell her, Chief?"

"Tell her that her Daddy's been in a boating accident."

"She's gonna want to know more than that, Chief," said Deputy Rhodes.

"We all want to know more than that," said Chief Rudolph. "But for now, that's all we really do know."

The Jensens' weren't the only family that had decided not to renew their brokerage agreement with Clayton Realty.

The Meelers', The Moshers', and The Burts' all had done the same. They all were stuck with homes they couldn't sell. Each family had dropped its asking price by thousands. But it wasn't enough. There were no buyers. None.

Except, maybe, one.

Deena Goode had been wistfully looking at real estate ads ever since the start of the school year. The commute from her apartment in Edgewater was over an hour each way and the miles were adding up quickly on her Volvo. Also, gas wasn't cheap. It would make sense to move closer, and it would be even nicer if she could find a house in Turtleback Lake. But Deena didn't have much in savings. Even with her new principal's salary, she thought it would take a couple years before she could afford a home in Turtleback Lake.

Then everything changed.

Prices in Turtleback Lake were in a free fall. No one wanted to buy a home in a town that had a giant snapper on the loose. But Deena was looking beyond the crisis. Somehow, somebody was going to remedy the situation. And as soon as that happened, prices would bounce right back up. Deena intended to get in while the getting in was good.

She'd been watching prices drop in the local paper. She also checked out the listings in the window of Clayton Realty – after Judd Clayton had gone home for the night. She had her eye on one particular listing: the Burts' bungalow.

Then one evening the Burts' bungalow was gone from the

window of Clayton Realty. Hardly believing her eyes, Deena drove past the house and saw it was true. The FOR SALE sign in front of the bungalow was gone.

"Dammit!" she muttered.

Deena could have kicked herself. She'd waited too long. The house was off the market.

Deena was beside herself. She should've acted. She should've made an offer. And she would have – if the Burts' home hadn't been listed with Clayton Realty. Because it was, she would have had to deal with Judd. And that would have been awfully awkward – for both of them. She knew Judd was angry. First she had given him the cold shoulder in the summer and then there'd been that unfortunate scene in front of the school council. Plus she sort of owed him for giving her the inside track on the principal job. Looking back, she guessed she could have handled the whole situation a lot better.

Now a golden opportunity had slipped through her fingers. The Burts' house – a lovely two-bedroom bungalow on the lake's western shore – would have been perfect for her. Not too big, not too small – with a wooden deck that looked out over the water. And best of all, it was just a short walk through the woods to the Andersen cabin.

Deena thought back to what August had said to her that night in the summer, after the two of them had gone through two bottles of wine. She remembered his exact words. He had told her that something was *"pulling him back to the lake."*

Could he have meant her?

And then, when she had asked August about extending her lease beyond September, he had declined. Was it because he secretly intended to be in it himself?

There are bobbers. And then there are sinkers.

Jack Sully was a bobber. Given a choice, Jack definitely would have chosen to be a sinker. That way the damn town would've had to do for him what they should've done for his daughter: dredge the lake.

How Jack's body got all the way from the middle of the lake to the grassy shallows in its northeast corner was a matter for speculation. Thermal currents were one theory. Breezes were another. Both were wrong.

The truth was, Jack – or the little that was left of him – had been dragged across the lake by Grundel.

Connie Konsulis had spotted the body from the deck of her house when she got home from her early morning jog. When Deputy Rhodes and Chief Rudolph arrived at her door, she led them out onto the deck so they could see for themselves.

"How do we get down there?" asked Chief Rudolph, looking at the steep drop down to the water.

"Follow me," she told him.

Rhodes and Rudolph followed Connie down the twisting, rocky path that plunged from her deck down to the lakeshore. Chief Rudolph stumbled twice. He should've kept his eyes on where his feet were going, but instead he kept sneaking peeks at Connie's sparkly pink running shorts. They weren't just short, pink, and sparkly; they were also clingy.

"All right, Donny," said the Chief when they reached the shoreline. "Wade out there and see what we've got."

Rhodes slipped off his shoes and socks and bunched up his trouser legs as far as they'd go. Then he waded through the willowy wisps of tall grass that grew up from the silty bottom. Twenty yards from shore, he came upon Jack's body, bobbing face down in the middle of the watery lawn.

"Jeez, Chief!" cried Deputy Rhodes.

All that was left of Jack Sully's body was his torso. His four limbs were gone.

Chief Rudolph turned to Connie.

"You stay here," he told her.

Then he bent over to remove his shoes and socks, hiked up his pants, and waded out to join Rhodes.

"Flip him over, Donny."

"Can't you?"

"Oh for chrissakes, Donny!"

Chief Rudolph reached down, grabbed a wet handful of what remained of Jack Sully's shirt, and rolled him over.

"Awww-christ!"

Both men had to look away.

All the parts that had once been between Jack's two legs were gone. Intestines and God-only-knew-what other entrails were dangling out of the gaping gash.

Chief Rudolph looked toward shore.

"Do you have some kind of tarp or blanket we could use?" he called to Connie. "Something you won't need back."

"I'll go get one," she called.

Connie turned and started climbing back up the hill. Chief Rudolph watched her in her clingy pink shorts. He regretted his eyes weren't better.

JJ was racing up the B-wing stairwell, taking two steps at a time, when Dr. Goode's voice came crackling through the school's public address system. She was summoning someone to her office, but JJ couldn't make out the name.

Maybe they've found whoever painted Turtleback Rock, he thought.

JJ emerged from the stairwell, turned right and bumped face first into someone coming down the hall. Binders, books and papers flew everywhere. Both students gasped.

It took a moment for JJ to realize whom he'd crashed into.

It was Mary.

"I'm so sorry," he said. "Are you okay?"

"I'm fine," said Mary. "How about you?"

"I'm okay, too," said JJ.

They both looked down at the floor. Papers were strewn everywhere.

"We better clean this up," said Mary with a laugh.

"Right," said JJ, kneeling down beside her.

JJ started collecting papers. On one sheet were Mary's English class notes on *Ethan Frome.* The margins of the page were filled with doodles – flowers, curlicues, and hearts. Inside one of the hearts, with an arrow through it, was the number 24.

Mary reached over.

"Thanks," she said, blushing. "That one's mine."

When they finally finished gathering together the last of the scattered papers and books, they stood and faced each other.

"Well, you better hurry," said Mary.

"You too," said JJ. "You don't want to miss your next period."

"I sure don't," said Mary, winking at JJ. "But don't you worry. I've only got study hall next. But you better hurry. Dr. Goode is waiting for you."

"Dr. Goode?" said JJ. "Waiting for me?"

"Didn't you hear the page?" asked Mary.

"I heard something," said JJ. "But it was all crackly."

"Well, it was Dr. Goode," said Mary. "And she was calling you to her office."

Mary suddenly lowered her voice and did her best imitation of Dr. Goode speaking through the P.A. system.

"Judd Clayton, Junior. Would you please report to the principal's office immediately."

"Well, I better go," said JJ. "See *ya!*"

"Yeah," said Mary. "See *ya!*"

* * *

"I'm sorry to have to call you down here again," said Dr. Goode, as JJ walked into her office. "But there's been another, um, incident. Police Chief Rudolph would like to see you again. There's a patrol car waiting for you out front."

JJ nodded and began to get up from his chair.

This was the second time Dr. Goode had called JJ to her office. She remembered studying his features closely the first time. He was a handsome boy, blonde haired, with beautiful pale green eyes. Yet he looked nothing like his father. She remembered thinking: he must take after his mother.

But now, as JJ turned to leave, something about his features struck her as strangely familiar. She knew this face – but from where? As unlikely as it seemed, could Deena have possibly crossed paths with – or even known – JJ's mother – the woman who Judd said ran out one morning and never came back?

* * *

Deputy Rhodes drove JJ down to the boat basin. Chief Rudolph was waiting for them. Jack Sully's canoe had been dragged up onto the dock, where its red metal hull was heating up in the warm autumnal sun.

Chief Rudolph greeted JJ with a nod.

"Thanks for coming, JJ. I'm sorry to have to drag you out of school, but there's been another incident. There's something we have to check out."

"Sure," said JJ. "What can I do?"

"If you'll come over here, I'll show you."

Chief Rudolph took JJ by the elbow and led him over to Jack Sully's canoe. They walked around to the side that JJ had been unable to see. There, on the port side, were jagged streaks: the canoe's bright red paint had been scraped off down to the shiny metal beneath. The metal itself had been deeply gouged – almost scored all the way through.

"If you don't mind, JJ," said the Chief. "I'd like to ask you to lift up your shirt."

"What for?" asked JJ.

"You'll see," said Chief Rudolph.

JJ pulled up his polo shirt. The claw marks that streaked across JJ's abdomen had begun to scab over with dried blood, but they still looked nasty and painful.

"JJ, again, I hope you don't mind, but I need to get photos of this. Could you please position yourself alongside the scratches on the canoe."

JJ understood immediately. You didn't need to be a forensics expert to see that the marks on the canoe and those on JJ's torso were identical.

"Well," said Chief Rudolph. "We've got ourselves a match."

It was strange being back. It was strange to be sleeping again in the cabin that his father and grandfather had built. And it was even stranger to think that the same monster that had mutilated his grandfather might still be alive and at large in Turtleback Lake.

Ever since he'd visited the cabin back in the summer, August had felt something pulling him back. And now, sure enough, here he was: back.

Back then – when was it – late June, early July? – August had let himself go too far with Deena. He should have left after their first bottle of wine. After their second, Deena had gone to the window and lowered the blinds, as if she didn't want the moon to look in. Then she had gone to the couch and patted the cushion next to her seductively.

August had tried to resist. He wanted Deena, but he knew it wasn't right. There had been times when, as a professor, he had felt similarly seduced by graduate or doctoral students. But he had always resisted. And now, maybe because Deena had shown him her dissertation, he viewed her as if she, too, were a student. It didn't matter that she was more-than-of-age and more-than-consenting. She was offering herself to him for the wrong reasons – because of his credentials and because she'd drunk too much. The fact was they'd both drunk too much.

The whole thing made August recall another incident he deeply regretted. It was something so bizarre and so out of character that August often tried to convince himself that it had never really happened.

It had been a late summer afternoon, probably fourteen or fifteen years ago now, and August had fallen asleep after swimming out to the floating dock. Suddenly the dock was jarred. Something had rammed against it. August woke with a start and looked around. A small sailboat was rocking alongside.

"Hi!" said a woman in the boat. August looked at her. She was blonde and very pretty, but there was also something wild, even crazy, about her eyes. All she was wearing was a pair of white shorts and a pink bikini top.

"Can I join you on your little isle for awhile?" she asked, already climbing up onto the dock.

August was caught completely off guard.

"Sure," he said, not knowing quite what to say. "Why not?"

Before August even knew what was happening, the woman had climbed on top of him and was straddling his hips. Then she began loosening her bikini top.

"Hey – wait a minute," said August. "What are you doing?"

But before August could say another word, the woman's mouth was on his. Her lips were sweet and wet. August sighed and surrendered.

A few minutes later, the woman rolled off him.

"Well," she said. "I guess I can cross *that* off my list."

"Your list?" said August.

"Yes," she said. "My list. You mean you don't have one?"

Then she turned and climbed back down into her boat. August didn't know her name and she hadn't asked for his. As she sailed away, she never once turned around.

August never mentioned the incident to anyone. He liked to

pretend it had never happened. But he knew it had. Sometimes he even thought it was the reason he chose to stay away from Turtleback Lake.

His one night with Deena had brought back the whole memory. But what could he do or say? There was no turning back the clock. And in this case – with the wine, the moonlight, and Deena's recumbent body laying on the couch with her half unbuttoned blouse – it all had been too much.

* * *

It was the middle of the night – the middle of August's first night sleeping in the cabin. He had left his window open to let in the cool night air.

August wasn't sure whether the loud crack he heard – the blast – was real or a dream. August always had vivid dreams when he slept somewhere new or different and the dream he'd been having was beyond vivid – it bordered on nightmarish.

August had been in a lab, strapped down to a cold examination table. Electrodes, taped to his abdomen, were connected to a monitor that August could see by raising his head. He watched a dome-shaped light move restlessly back and forth across the bottom of the screen, like a creature scavenging the seabed. As it moved, it blinked and beeped softly.

Then the dome-shaped light began to rise. It caromed from one side to the other, each ricochet sending it closer to the top of the monitor. As it rose, it began to flash brighter and beep louder. Now for the first time August could see there was another light on the screen, bobbing up near the top. Suddenly the dome-shaped light seemed to zero in on it. Beeping wildly, it shot like a heat-seeking missile straight toward the bobbing light. A second later it engulfed it and then burst with a blast into tiny sparks that rained slowly back down to the bottom of the screen.

At the sound of the blast, August awoke and sat straight up. The air coming through the window felt cool against the beads of sweat on his brow.

August threw off the covers and walked over to the window. Standing there, looking out at the moon-glazed lake, he almost imagined he could feel the last vibrations of an echo that had just died in the valley outside. Suddenly the surface of the lake went black. August looked up at the sky. An immense cloud was blotting out the moon.

August went back to bed. He reached over and turned off the alarm clock. He'd sleep in.

But at 7:00 a.m., a persistent ring awakened August. Forgetting that he had turned off the alarm clock during the night, he reached over to silence it. But the ringing didn't stop. Then he realized it was the phone.

He lifted up the heavy black receiver, the one that Deena had used as a dumbbell.

"Hello," he said.

"August!" said the voice on the other end. "This is Chief Rudolph. Sorry to spoil your first morning back in town, but if you don't mind, there's something I'd like you to come see."

"Where?" asked August.

"Down at the town morgue," answered Chief Rudolph.

"I'll be there in twenty minutes," said August. Then he hung up the phone.

"So, hot shot," said Coach Lupo. "You think you're pretty funny, don't you?"

Coach Lupo's face had never been this close to his before. Kenny wanted to pull his head back, but he didn't dare. And Lupo's piercing blue eyes wouldn't let him look away. Kenny could see all the little red blood vessels branching across Coach Lupo's eye whites. He could smell the stale coffee on his coach's breath.

"It's funny to mock the way a man walks behind his back, right Lubowsky?"

Lubowsky felt unable to speak. He could hardly believe what was happening. For three years, Coach Lupo had liked him.

"I said it's funny to ridicule a cripple, am I right?"

Lubowsky tried to shake his head from side to side without taking his eyes off Coach Lupo's.

"I want to tell you a little something you don't know. You think you're a pretty good halfback, right?"

Lubowsky said nothing.

"I said, you think you're a pretty good halfback, right?"

Lubowsky made a sound that wasn't quite a word.

"Well, let me tell you something. You're not *half* the halfback Oscar Hall was when he was a young man. In fact, you're not an *eighth* of the halfback he was. So what would that make you? A sixteenth? A thirty-second?"

Coach Lupo's face was still too close to his. And now Kenny was having trouble following Coach Lupo's math.

"When Oscar Hall was a boy," continued the coach, "he was faster, stronger, and smarter than you'll ever be. And he didn't think he was God's gift to the world every time he broke a few tackles and scored. He didn't make a spectacle of himself with some look-at-me-I'm-the-man shimmy shimmy victory dance. He'd just flip the ball back to the ref, return to the huddle, and get ready to block for the kicker."

Coach Lupo paused. Kenny hoped he was finished. But he wasn't.

"You, young man, are never going to approach the player he was, let alone the man. So when I see someone like you making a mockery of a man whose shoes you're not fit to shine, well, it kind of makes me want to puke. How about you, Lubowsky? Doesn't it kind of make you want to puke, too?"

Suddenly, Kenny *did* feel like puking. And it was coming up from inside of him faster than he could stop it. For a brief instant, his cheeks bulged. Then the puke was all over. Kenny had had a big breakfast that morning. Now it was all over him, the floor, and Coach Lupo's desk.

"For chrissakes, Lubowsky, go clean yourself up."

Coach Lupo waited until Lubowsky was out of his sight. Then he let his mind drift back to a summer night almost a half-century earlier – a night when he had convinced Oscar to go out onto the lake with him. Their canoe had been swamped by something they never saw. They couldn't get the canoe back upright, because something kept ramming it. They had started swimming to shore as fast as they could. When they were almost there, Oscar had screamed. Bill had never heard anything like that scream before. Something had bitten Oscar's ankle – right through his Achilles to the bone. Oscar was never the same again, never scored another touchdown, never got the scholarship he surely would have gotten. Oscar had never blamed Bill for what had happened that night. He had never said a word about it.

Bill Lupo picked up the phone on his desk. He dialed the boiler room extension.

"Oscar, it's me, Bill. I hate to ask you this, but some kid just puked his guts out in my office. Could you bring me up a mop and some ammonia? The joint stinks. Thanks."

Deena could hardly believe her eyes. Flipping through the pages of *The Bergen Record*, she spotted an ad for the house she thought had gotten away.

It was a "For Sale By Owner" ad. The Burts' were going to try to sell their house by themselves. Deena called the number and said she'd like to stop by.

"It's nice," said Deena, after Shirley Burt had led her on a little tour of the bungalow and property. "Of course it needs a bit of work."

Deena didn't want to sound *too* enthusiastic. Though the Burts' had already reduced their price dramatically, Deena thought she might be able to get them down even lower. While showing Deena around, Shirley had let it slip that she and her husband had already closed on a townhouse in a retirement community in North Carolina. They'd need the money from this house to help pay for that one.

"As I said, I really like it," said Deena. "But I'll need a little time to think it over."

It was a bit of a ploy, but Deena thought maybe they'd knock another thousand or two off the price just to keep her from walking out the door.

"Of course, dear," said Shirley, not wanting to pressure the younger woman. "Just give us a call when you've made up your mind."

That had been on Sunday. The Burts' thought that they might hear back later that day – or the next day at the latest. Now it was Thursday and still there'd been no word from Dr. Goode.

Frank Burt had gone into town. Now he was walking through the front door with a copy of *The Turtleback Gazette* in his hand.

"Look at this honey," he said, holding open the newspaper for his wife to see.

Shirley looked at the front page. She didn't have her glasses on but she didn't need them. The headline was huge.

TURTLE TERROR!

Major newspapers throughout New Jersey picked up the article, written by Marc Bozian. It showed up in *The Star Ledger, The Bergen Record,* even *The Asbury Park Press.* The story's appearance on the front page of the metro section of *The New York Times* was the biggest feather yet in the young journalist's career.

THIRD AND WORST TURTLE ATTACK
SHOCKS RESIDENTS OF LAKE COMMUNITY!

Marc Bozian's article more than satisfied readers' appetites for grisly details. It also saw the attack as part of a disturbing, escalating trend: first a toe, then a limb, now a quadruple amputation resulting in the death of the first victim's father.

Bozian quoted Connie Konsulis, the woman who had first spotted the body floating in the lake.

"From the deck of my house," said Ms. Konsulis, age 36, "it kind

of looked like a suitcase or a piece of luggage that had washed ashore." Connie was such a pretty witness that the paper decided to include a picture of her out on her deck in her pink running shorts. The paper also included the photograph of JJ's scars paired with the claw marks on the canoe. The article left very little doubt that the attacks were by the same giant snapper.

Chief Rudolph, however, was not entirely convinced. *"Maybe the last two attacks,"* he was quoted as saying, *"but I'm not sure about the little girl's toe. In comparison to the others, a toe is nothing – a regular ordinary snapper could've done it."*

Before his wife could even get through the first paragraph, Frank Burt blurted out, "This is the last thing we needed. Let's call that woman and try to light a fire under her."

Deena had given the Burts' her number both at home and at school. Shirley looked at the clock on the wall and then dialed the school extension.

"Sorry to bother you at work," said Shirley. "But we were wondering what you were thinking about the house. Maybe it would help if you stopped by for a second look."

"Sure," said Deena. "I'll come by after school today. Is four-thirtyish alright?"

Deena showed up at quarter to five. Shirley and Frank gave her the tour together this time. When they were done, Shirley invited Deena to sit down for the tea and biscuits she had set out hoping to soften Deena up.

"Look," said Deena. "I love your little house. But I have to be honest. I'm not sure if now is a good time to be buying a house here. Did you see today's paper?"

The Burts' exchanged a glance. Their hopes fell.

"It might just make better sense," said Deena, "for me to wait a little. There are a number of houses on the market now and prices

159

could come down even lower. I might find a better deal elsewhere."

Frank cut Deena off.

"What if we took another twenty-thousand off the price?"

Shirley Burt gasped. She and her husband had not discussed a further price cut.

"I don't know, Frank," said Shirley. "At that price, we'd barely be breaking even."

Frank ignored his wife. He kept his eyes on Deena.

"It's a limited-time-only offer," he said.

"When does it end?" asked Deena.

"Soon."

"How soon?" asked Deena

"The moment you step through that doorway," said Frank.

Deena looked from Frank to the door to Shirley.

"All right," she said. "You've got a deal. I'll take it."

Deena put out her hand. Frank shook it. Shirley didn't say anything. She was too shocked to speak.

When August arrived at the morgue, what was left of Jack Sully was strapped on a slab so it wouldn't roll off.

"So what do you think, August?" said the Chief. "You're the town's resident scientific expert – at least for as long as you're *in* town."

Chief Rudolph said "in town" as if he thought August was perfectly capable of leaving Turtleback Lake before he even finished his sentence.

But August didn't take the bait. He just said what he thought.

"Well, I think it's pretty obvious that this was done by the same snapper that got Ian Copeland and my grandfather," said August. "Unless…"

"Unless what?" asked Chief Rudolph.

"Unless there's more than one," said August. "Or this snapper is a descendant of the one who attacked my grandfather. We can't be a hundred percent certain."

"Well, that's encouraging," said Chief Rudolph. "Let's just hope there's only one – whether it's the same one that got your grand-daddy or a newer model."

Both men were silent for a moment. August looked at the stumps that protruded from the bottom of Jack Sully's torso. They looked like hams with the bone still in. Both legs had been sheered off just inches below the hip. The gruesome gash between the stumps was mercifully covered with a cloth. August didn't bother to lift it.

"So, what do you think, August?" said Chief Rudolph. "Any ideas on how we go about killing this thing?"

August tilted his head like a bird and looked at Chief Rudolph.

"I don't think killing it should be our goal," said August.

"Oh, really?" said Chief Rudolph. "What do you think our goal should be?"

"I think our goal should be to catch it," said August, ignoring the sarcasm that had come suddenly into Chief Rudolph's voice.

"Oh, c'mon, August! This thing is a killer, a man-eater. It's murdered, maimed, and mutilated. Ever read scripture?"

August raised his eyebrows, unsure where Chief Rudolph's sudden religious turn was heading.

"Some," said August.

"Well then you might've read, 'As yea sow, so shall yea reap.'"

"You're applying standards of human morality to a creature

that isn't human."

"That's a crock of bull!" said Chief Rudolph. "If a pit bull attacks a person, what do we do with it? Pat it on the head and say 'nice doggy?' Hell, no, we put it to sleep – permanent sleep!"

"Not even everybody agrees with that," said August.

Chief Rudolph felt his outrage rising. Was August some kind of goddam egghead pacifist?

"And it's not an apt comparison," continued August. "Dogs become aggressive because of the people who raise them."

This was too much! Chief Rudolph was in no mood for a philosophical *tête-à-tête* with an Ivy League professor.

"Listen, Andersen," he said. "People didn't make this turtle into a killer. Nobody's ever done anything to him. He was born evil and he's going to die evil – and the sooner the better!"

"I don't know, Chief," said August. He had an academic's habit of turning everything over and looking at it from another side. And an odd little detail – one that he had never thought about – had suddenly just occurred to him.

"What about Ted Tanner?" said August. "And what the players on the football team do to those snappers?"

For a brief moment, Chief Rudolph was speechless. Nobody ever talked about what went on with the freshman football players. It wasn't done – it was taboo. Frankly, he was surprised Andersen even knew about it.

"What the hell are you suggesting?" said Chief Rudolph, now practically shouting. "That this snapper's attacks are some kind of revenge? Or that they're somehow justified?"

"No, Chief, I'm not saying that," said August in a voice that only made Chief Rudolph angrier. "I guess I was just thinking aloud. What I do believe, however, is this creature should be caught – not killed. It could turn out to be the largest snapper ever in captivity.

It might be a mutant or a leftover from the prehistoric past – like the coelacanth."

"The *what?*" said Chief Rudolph.

"The coelacanth," repeated August. "It was a fish thought to be extinct for millions of years – until one was caught in the Indian Ocean back in the nineteen thirties."

"Forget all that *BS*," said Rudolph. "You're putting science ahead of people's lives."

"No, I'm not," said August. "If the snapper's in captivity, it's as good as killing it. It'll be out of the lake and people will be safe."

"That's going to be a hard sell to the people of this town," said Chief Rudolph.

"Then why tell them?" said August.

There were signs posted at every access point along the lakeshore: *No Swimming or Boating Until Further Notice By Order of The Turtleback Lake Police Department.*

And, in at least one sense, nature was helping out.

The long hot summer that seemed to have stretched all the way into October had finally come to an end. Evening temperatures were dropping into the low 40s and upper 30s. In the morning, mists rose off the lake and hung like a ghostly fog until the sun came over the mountains and burned it away. In a week, the temperature of the water in the lake dropped almost twenty degrees. Nobody was going to be tempted to defy Chief Rudolph's ban on swimming – the water was just too cold.

Boaters were another story. Some argued that Jack Sully's death was due largely to his inebriation. The whole incident could've been avoided if he'd been sober.

"Drunk or sober, nobody's going out on that lake till this thing's resolved," said Chief Rudolph. And for the time being, nobody pushed the issue. A few boat owners grumbled, but they all complied.

And then, just as Chief Rudolph feared, August Andersen was gone.

Chief Rudolph was ticked off. For whatever reason, he had secretly viewed August as Turtleback Lake's white knight. Despite their differing viewpoints, Chief Rudolph had ceded some authority to Andersen because of his scientific expertise. He was confident August was working on some kind of plan to catch the snapper. And if he could catch it before anyone else could kill it, well then, good riddance. The beast would be out of the lake and everyone would be safe.

And then – *poof!* – August was gone.

For three straight mornings Chief Rudolph had called Andersen, but got no answer. You'd have thought the guy would have voice mail or at least an answering machine, but no – all he had was a vintage rotary phone that did nothing but ring and ring and ring.

"Goddammit!" cursed Rudolph, slamming down his phone. Then he had a thought that gave him a glimmer of hope: maybe Andersen simply had turned off the ringer.

Rudolph hopped in his car and drove out to Andersen's cabin. First he pounded on the door with his fist. Then he peered through the windows. There was nothing: *nada* Andersen, *nada* car, *nada* nothing. The guy was gone – again.

"Why am I even surprised?" said the Chief when he got back to the station. "Why did I even *think* Andersen was going to help us? The guy's been a phantom for years! Why should we expect anything from him now?"

"I don't know, Chief," said Deputy Rhodes. "Because of his special expertise?"

"Exactly, Rhodes," said the Chief, shocked to hear his deputy say exactly what he himself was thinking. "The town needs his special expertise. His departure isn't a disappearance – it's a...it's a...."

"A desertion?" offered Deputy Rhodes.

"Exactly," said the Chief. "It's a desertion. A dereliction of duty."

* * *

But August was gone – and nobody knew where.

While he was away, Deena closed on the Burt bungalow. It happened quickly – in a matter of days. Then, in every free moment she had, Deena began readying the cabin for moving in. After school and on weekends, she scrubbed, swept, scoured and scraped.

Then, one Friday, Deena spent her first night in her new home – in a sleeping bag rolled out on the floor. Her plan was to get an early start on Saturday morning. She had rollers, brushes, drop cloths, step ladders, pans and a couple cans of Sherwin Williams dove white. She was going to give the walls a clean fresh coat.

In the morning, Deena was up with the sun. She was eating a bagel and drinking a cup of coffee when she heard the crunch of gravel in the drive outside. She went to the window and pulled aside the curtain.

A Volvo was driving by – August's Volvo! Back in the summer, Deena had noticed that he drove the exact same model and year as she did. It was a coincidence that Deena felt meant something – like maybe they were made for each other.

Behind the Volvo was a trailer. August was towing something, but she couldn't see what. Whatever it was, it was under a tarp.

Deena waved and called through the screened window, but the car rolled past without stopping. Apparently, August hadn't heard her.

Deena couldn't repress her immediate desire to see him. She put the lid back on the gallon of primer she'd just opened and stirred. She was glad she hadn't dipped her brush in yet. She went to the bathroom, gave herself a quick glance in the mirror then walked the short distance between her bungalow and August's cabin.

August had just started untying the tarp that covered the trailer.

"Hi, stranger," Deena called.

August spun around, dropping the corner of the tarp that he'd just lifted.

"Hey, hi!" he said, surprised to see Deena in painter's pants and hat. "What are you doing here on a Saturday morning?"

"Oh, I just came by to see if I could borrow a cup of sugar."

August looked perplexed.

"A cup of sugar?" he repeated.

"Isn't that what neighbors do?" said Deena. "Borrow cups of sugar."

Andersen raised an eyebrow.

"Neighbors?" he repeated.

"I just closed on the Burt bungalow," she told him. "It happened while you were away."

"Well, that's news." said August. "Congratulations. Were you serious about a cup of sugar?"

"No, I was just kidding. But I wouldn't say no to a cup of coffee."

"Sure," said August. "Come on in. I'll make some."

While August set up the coffee maker, Deena went to the window where she had spent countless hours writing. It was funny. She had come to Turtleback Lake to get away from men and she had failed miserably. Yet she couldn't have been happier.

Then she looked out at the lake – first at the white rock out in the middle and then at the wooden dock that floated forty or fifty yards from shore. She thought back on the many times she had swum out to it. She'd been lucky. *She* could've been one of the snapper's victims.

But now she felt certain that nothing was going to get her. Somebody was going to get the beast out of the lake and she had a feeling that it was going to be August – *her* August. He didn't know it yet, but he was going to be hers. Just as *he* was going to catch that snapper, *she* was going to catch him.

"How do you like it?" said August.

Deena was still looking out the window with her back to him. "It's beautiful," answered Deena.

"I meant your coffee," said August. "How do you take it?"

"A little milk, no sugar. Thanks."

She was waiting for August to say, "Sugar? You're sweet enough without it."

But August wasn't a dispenser of clichés. He simply opened the refrigerator and took out a carton of milk. He put his nose to it.

"*P-U!*" he said. "I'm sorry, but the milk's gone bad. Would black be okay?"

"As long as it's hot and strong," she said.

August handed the coffee to Deena. She wrapped her fingers around the mug and inhaled the steam rising off it.

"So – what are you towing?" she asked, nodding through the window at the trailer outside. "It looks so long and tubular. It's not a submarine, is it?"

"Actually, I was hoping to keep it secret," said August.

Deena waited, hoping August would share his secret with her.

"It's an SV," he said finally.

"Excuse me?" said Deena.

"Sorry," said August. "It's an SV – a submersible vessel. It's really just a small two-man sub."

"You're not thinking about taking it out on the lake?"

"Of course I am," said August.

"What if this giant snapper attacks you?"

"That's what I'm counting on," said August. "I'm hoping I can lure him close enough to capture."

"Anyone else in on this plan? It sounds dangerous."

"Nope," said August. "This is a solo mission."

"Don't you think Chief Rudolph should know?" said Deena. "So he can provide some kind of backup?"

August shook his head.

"Chief Rudolph and I see things differently," said August. "He wants the turtle dead. I want it captured – so it can be studied."

"Well, I can see the advantage of your position," said Deena. "But I don't know about the rest of the town. There's a real blood lust in the air."

"Well, you know what the Chinese say," said August. "When you set out for revenge, dig two graves."

"I don't think I understand," said Deena.

"One grave for the person you're seeking revenge against," explained August. "And another one for yourself."

"Well, I just think you should be careful," said Deena. "And anyway, don't you think Chief Rudolph will eventually find out what you're up to?"

"I don't think so," said August. "Where I'm going, no one – including Chief Rudolph – will see me."

It was late October. Halloween was drawing near.

For years, snapping turtle costumes had been a big hit in Turtleback Lake. Tons of kids wore them. But this year – in light of the recent tragic events – many people thought they'd be in poor taste.

Parents especially were opposed to them. But kids wanted to wear them as much as ever. This year they'd *really* be scary! And for younger children whose older siblings had worn them in the past, it seemed unfair. This year was their turn.

On Halloween night, more than a few parents gave in.

"Okay, you can be a snapping turtle," many said. "But whatever you do, don't go trick-or-treating at The Copelands' house wearing that costume."

Nobody had to worry about trick-or-treating at The Sully house.

After Jack Sully's death, little Joanne had been picked up and whisked away to live with an aunt from somewhere down in South Jersey. The Sully house stood vacant – dark and deserted. On Halloween night, it looked like the closest thing to a real haunted house that Turtleback Lake had ever seen. Loose shutters banged in the wind, dead leaves skittered across the front porch, branches scratched against blackened windows. Kids crossed to the other side of the street just to avoid it.

Up in the Skytop section, trick-or-treaters were scarce. Because of multi-acre zoning, homes were few and far between. Unless you lived in the neighborhood, it wasn't worth the trek. The Claytons' doorbell had hardly rung all evening.

Still, JJ sat in a chair in the front hall, just in case anyone did show up. The plastic pumpkin head on the little table next to him was still brimming with Butterfingers and fun-size bags of peanut M&Ms. JJ and his dad would be eating them for weeks to come.

JJ looked at his watch. It was 9:30. He closed the book he was reading. Maybe it was time to close shop.

Then, as he reached for the switch to turn off the front door light, a loud hard knock startled him. JJ jumped. He looked through one of the two windows that flanked the door. Someone was out there: a tall kid dressed as a pirate. The kid had a patch over one eye, a black bandanna patterned with skulls and cross-bones, and a stuffed parrot perched on his shoulder. JJ swung open the door.

"*Aaargh, matey!*" hailed the pirate in a deep throaty voice. "Any booty for a buccaneer with a peg leg?"

JJ almost knocked the pirate over with a bear hug.

"Ian! It's so good to see you! Come on in!"

Ian Copeland stumped into the entry hall. It was the first time JJ had seen Ian in weeks. He tried not to look down at the prosthetic device that was Ian's new right foot.

"So how's it going?" asked Ian. "And how's the team?"

Ian had been away for more than three weeks at a physical rehabilitation center.

"Forget about me and the team," said JJ. "How are you?"

"Believe it or not, I'm fine," said Ian. "I saw stuff while I was away that kind of put things in perspective."

"What do you mean?" asked JJ.

"This place I was at," said Ian. "There were people there – old people, young people, even little kids. And the things they'd been through you wouldn't want to know. Some had no legs, let alone one foot. And yet none of them complained. So how could I?"

Then Ian walked back and forth across the entry hall.

"What do you think about my new gait?" asked Ian.

"You can hardly tell you're limping," said JJ.

"Well, that's not true," said Ian. "But enough about me. Tell me about the team!"

"Well, we're still undefeated," said JJ. "But we've had a couple of real squeakers. We've missed you, Ian."

"Who's been doing the kicking?" asked Ian.

JJ knew the question was going to come. The answer to it had been eating away at him for weeks.

"Well," said JJ. "For the last two games, I have."

Ian didn't even flinch.

"That's great!" he said. "I didn't know you could."

"Neither did I," said JJ. "But one day, as I was running out onto the practice field, a soccer ball rolled in front of me. I kicked it. I was surprised at how far it went. Lupo saw me and made me kick it again. Then he made me try a few place kicks. I wasn't bad. It's probably from watching you do it so many times."

"It's probably from all those bike races we had coming home from practice," said Ian. "You've got legs of steel."

Ian reached down and tapped the ankle of his new prosthetic foot. It clinked.

"Then again," he laughed, "so do I!"

Dr. Goode had been wrong about who had defaced Turtleback

Rock. It wasn't a student – or students – at Turtleback High.

It was an alumnus, class of '80.

There were no eyewitnesses, but the circumstantial evidence was as damning as any testimony could possibly be. First there were the dried splatters and drippings of paint found on the side of Jack Sully's canoe: yellow, black, red and white – the same four colors used to paint the cartoon snapper on Turtleback Rock.

Then there were the empty paint cans found in Jack's garage. The empty cans included the same four colors. But the nails in Jack's coffin had been the crude sketches Chief Rudolph found on a table inside Jack's house: sketches of a stick figure person holding a paintbrush while standing on the dome of a turtle's back.

"I didn't know Jack had so much talent," Chief Rudolph said to Deputy Rhodes flipping through the sketches. "Some of these aren't half-bad."

Of course there would be no day in court for Jack. He was already incarcerated in a custom-made half-size pinewood coffin buried six-feet deep in Turtleback Rock Cemetery. The grave marker was cheap and simple: a large boulder that had been painted white.

Deena knew she had been wrong in accusing her students of a crime that none of them had committed. The November issue of *The Mosaic*, the high school's monthly newspaper, gave her a chance to make amends.

The person responsible for the defacement of Turtleback Rock has been found. The perpetrator was a local house painter, the same unfortunate man who died in the most recent snapping turtle attack. While his crime was offensive, his passing is a tragedy as it has made an orphan of his innocent daughter. The silver lining in this dark cloud is that all suspicions leveled against the students of this school – including my own – have been proved baseless.

Marc Bozian seized on the same topic for a short piece on the opinion page of *The Turtleback Gazette*. Marc wrote:

Though the perpetrator is dead, his crime lives on. Daily we are faced with the garish spectacle of Mr. Sully's last paint job, a sight that is all the more offensive given that it is such a vivid reminder of the even greater menace that still lurks in the waters beneath. Perhaps if our community could find a way to expunge this surface blight, we might be inspired to eliminate its objective correlative.

Marc wondered if he was using too many big words. But Marc liked big words. People could always look them up. That's why there were dictionaries.

He handed the finished piece to Michael Schneiderman to review.

Bozian watched Schneiderman's eyes tracking back and forth across the page. Then Michael looked up perplexed.

"What the heck does '*objective correlative*' mean?"

"It's when one thing stands for something else," explained Marc.

"So what's the objective correlative in your piece?"

"The snapping turtle is the objective correlative of the painted rock," explained Marc. Then he paused. Could he possibly have that backwards? Marc wasn't completely sure. But what did it matter? If *a* equals *b* then *b* equals *a*. The order didn't matter. It was the commutative property. Or maybe it was the associative property.

"Don't you think it's just a bit over our readers' heads?" asked Michael.

Bozian shrugged his shoulders. Schneiderman handed the article back to him.

"What the heck – just run it," said Schneiderman.

* * *

"It's ridiculous," said Judd.

Judd was sitting in a booth at Bonds' across from Michael Schneiderman. *The Turtleback Gazette* was spread open between them.

"People are talking as if removing the paint from Turtleback Rock is going to solve our problem," said Judd. "The real problem goes much deeper."

"You're missing the whole point of the piece," said Michael. "The point is the rock is just the tip of the iceberg. It's like a pimple, Judd. You've got to pop it to get the pus out."

"So what are you saying?" asked Judd. "That the graffiti on the rock is the pimple and the giant snapper is the pus and if we scrape the paint off the rock that will get rid of the snapper in the lake?"

That *was* what Michael meant. Though now that someone else was saying it, it sounded pretty preposterous. Maybe he was giving Bozian too much leeway.

"Well, a pimple is probably a bad analogy," said Michael. "But it's essentially what Bozian was driving at. If we take care of what is relatively a little problem we might be inspired to address the bigger one."

"You mean the 'objective correlative?'"

"All right, Judd," said Michael. "You know what I'm saying."

"Look, Mike," said Judd. "I want Turtleback Rock cleaned up as much as anyone. But it's been weeks now since Sully died and has anything at all been done about this turtle? No!"

Schneiderman shrugged his shoulders.

"I'll tell you what," said Judd. "I think people are actually starting to think that maybe this whole thing will just go away on its own. They're thinking that pretty soon the lake's gonna freeze and then – come spring when it thaws – everything will be fine again. And everything will be fine again – until it happens again."

The water in Turtleback Lake was cold, but August hardly felt it. He was wearing a wet suit. In any case, he wouldn't be in the water long. He only had to wade out a few more yards before climbing up the side of his sub and lowering himself into its open hatch.

Once inside, August sealed the hatch above, switched on the ignition, and surveyed the illuminated gauges on the instrument panel. As the vessel slipped past the floating dock, August flipped two more switches and the nose of the sub dipped beneath the surface. An instant later there was no sign of August or his sub.

In the predawn darkness, the surface of the lake was still jet black and its depths inkier still. Not until he was twenty feet down did August turn on the submarine's headlamps. Soon the sun would rise and lighten the eastern sky. Now that he was well under, August welcomed it. Sunlight on the lake's surface would prevent anyone from seeing the beam of his headlight probing beneath.

The actual depths of Turtleback Lake had never been charted. Who cared how deep a lake was when all its leisure activities took place on the surface? Turtleback Lake wasn't a Great Lake; it wasn't a shipping channel where vessels had to worry about running aground. The vessels that plied the waters of Turtleback Lake were canoes, rowboats, sailboats, kayaks, and inner tubes. Their hulls barely broke the surface.

Now August was once again in the uncharted underwater world he had loved exploring as a child. It was a filmy green realm filled with boundless wonder and potential danger. Who knew what the intrepid explorer might encounter if he dared to venture a tad too far or a foot too deep?

Through the thick glass of his vision panel, August peered into the waters lit by his searchlight. He glanced at his watch. It was 7 a.m. The sun was now high enough for him to turn on the craft's auxiliary lights.

Visibility straight ahead was about twenty feet, but August's peripheral vision was minimal. Eerie, sword-like bodies of deep-dwelling pikes and pickerels – fierce, prehistoric-looking things – darted across his field of vision.

This was the medium through which Grundel roamed like a lord, the unchallenged king of the food chain. He was the predator of all and the prey of none. He felt impervious and impregnable. Other than that nasty ax that had split his shell, nothing had caused Grundel the slightest pain in the last eighty years.

Well, every reign must end, mused August, thinking of the giant turtle's long dominance of the depths of Turtleback Lake.

Soon, if all went well, the turtle would be in an aquarium behind thick walls of tempered glass where – *where what?* August wondered. Would capturing the giant snapper be a boon to science? God knows he would love the chance to study such a creature. Or would the beast end up as a freakish tourist attraction? When there was a profit to be made, what wasn't turned into a circus spectacle?

August brought his focus back to the illuminated waters just beyond his windshield. Local legend was right: Turtleback Lake was as deep as the mountains around it. Once beyond the shallows ringing its shoreline, the sides plunged steeply downward, as if the basin of the lake were an upside-down hollowed-out mountain.

Where was Grundel's lair in this vast underwater world? Did

he roam the entire lake from end to end and shore to shore? Ian Copeland had been attacked in the lake's northeast corner off a dock in front of Judd Clayton's place. Joanne Sully was attacked at the public beach in the lake's southwest corner. And Jack Sully had been out in the middle. It seemed to August that this snapper was a roamer.

August wasn't sure that there was a best way to go about his search, so he let himself be guided by instinct and intuition. He dialed the nose of his sub in the direction of Turtleback Rock. In all his dives as a child, he had never gone anywhere near it. First of all, his father had issued a strict injunction against it. And then there had been the strange ominous aura that surrounded the rock. Even he, a child of logic and science, had felt it and respected it.

Turtleback Rock had always appeared – at least until Jack Sully got to it – as a low, slightly domed, bone-white island.

But in reality, the tiny island was actually a mountaintop – the tip of a mighty Gilbraltar whose precipitous sides plunged for hundreds of feet to the lake's bottom. If Turtleback Rock hadn't been ninety-nine per cent submerged, it would've been a mecca for rock climbers.

Suddenly, the water began to glow a spectral white. The beams of August's headlamps were reflecting off the sides of Turtleback Rock. As the sub neared the massive monolith, August veered to the left and began a clockwise circumnavigation.

Orbiting the white behemoth in his tiny tin tube, August felt like an astronaut on an early Mercury space mission. Growing up, August had regarded men like John Glenn as heroes. In his impressionable young mind, he had always imagined a second Mt. Rushmore carved with the faces of those early space travelers. That's the kind of monument young August dreamed about: a monument to intrepid men of science, adventure and exploration.

Now, as he rounded the bends of Turtleback Rock, August beheld new vistas of stunning beauty. It was like being immersed inside the globe of a giant paperweight.

August kept glancing at his gauges. They told him his depth, the pressure, the water temperature, and how much fuel and oxygen he had left. He had enough oxygen for ninety minutes more. He kept the nose of the sub pitched slightly downward, so as the craft was orbiting it constantly corkscrewed deeper and deeper.

At approximately two hundred feet, August noticed a large cave-like cavity in the side of the mountain. August estimated the opening to be twelve feet across and roughly eight feet high. It was shaped like a cartoon drawing of a caveman's home. The top and sides were arched, the floor was flat. August aligned the sub just outside the cave, pointed the nose inward, and adjusted the headlights to maximum luminosity.

August had expected the opening to be a shallow niche or alcove. What he saw instead was the entrance to a tunnel that looked big enough to accommodate a Cadillac. As far as August could see, the tunnel went straight in, ramping down ever so slightly. And, for at least as far as his headlamps revealed, the tunnel was wide enough for August to turn the sub around. If worse came to worst, he thought, I could always put it in reverse and back out: tricky, but do-able.

He took a deep breath and then plunged in. The capsule gave a small lurch and then began to slide into the open mouth of the cave.

All went smoothly for a while. The sub burrowed effortlessly, deeper and deeper into the bowels of the giant white rock. Then the tunnel, which had started so straight and wide, began to twist and turn, rise and fall. The gentle undulations didn't concern August until he suddenly became aware that the tunnel was also narrowing. A sudden wave of claustrophobia sped up his heart and quickened his breathing.

If I get wedged going around one of these bends, thought August, *Turtleback Rock is going to end up being my tombstone. And no one will ever know it.*

August put the craft into neutral and looked again at the glowing gauges on the instrument panel. He had lost track of time. More than half an hour had passed since he had last checked his oxygen supply. He had less than thirty minutes left now. And he still had to back out of the tunnel. Going any further was now out of the question. The possibility that an exit might be just around the next bend was a risk he couldn't take. He had to start backing out.

August took a deep breath. It didn't matter that it used up extra oxygen. Right now what he needed was to calm himself. Staying calm now could be the difference between life and death.

August adjusted the craft's rearview mirrors. He flicked a switch. The sub's taillights shot a beam into the blackness behind him. He shifted into reverse. Going backwards was slow going. Several times the sub bumped and scraped noisily against the stony sides. But August couldn't rush. He couldn't risk smashing a lamp, losing a mirror, or busting a sensor. What were the words his mother had drummed into his head as a boy? He could see them embroidered on a pillow. *Haste makes waste.* Going slow was the fastest way out.

August finally reached a point where the tunnel looked wide enough to attempt a three-point turn. He glanced at the gauge for oxygen. Twelve minutes left.

"Here goes nothing," he said.

August turned the wheel all the way to the left, easing the sub backward until it bumped against the wall behind him. The contact was jarring. Then he swung the wheel all the way back to the right and shifted forward. It was like trying to get out of a tight parking space in New York City. Sometimes you just couldn't. The side of the sub screeched as the metal scraped against the wall, but nothing broke off. August let out a breath. He was in the clear.

A few minutes later, August was out of the cave and on his way back to the surface. Turtleback Rock had almost gotten him – not by anything that it had done, but because of his own questionable judgment.

Chapter 24

Turtleback Lake November 2006

IT LOOKED LIKE IT would turn out to be a perfect day for a high school football game. The morning air was crisp, the rising sun was warm, and the sky was cloudless and blue.

It was 9 o'clock. August was having coffee in the kitchen when he heard a knock at the door.

August looked through the screen. He saw a woman in a black turtleneck, tight black stretch pants, and red sneakers with wide white laces. His new next door neighbor had come to pay a call.

August looked at her for a moment.

Only one thing gave away Deena's age – the crows' feet that creased the corners of her eyes whenever she smiled. But lines didn't matter to August. He actually preferred things a little aged, a little broken-in. And to his taste, Deena was just right. She looked good.

"Hey!" said Deena through the screen. "Good morning."

"And a good morning to you," said August, stepping outside.

"So," said Deena, letting out a sigh. "The reason I stopped by was to see if you might consider escorting a certain young lady to today's big game."

"Today's big game?" said August.

"The Snappers are playing the Ramapo Rams," said Deena. "Both teams are undefeated. I gather it's a big deal. The whole town's going."

"And who might be the young lady in need of an escort?" inquired August.

"She'd be me," said Deena with a sheepish smile.

August had to give her credit. She certainly put herself out there.

"Sure," said August. "It'd be my pleasure. What time?"

"Kick-off's at eleven," said Deena, exhaling with relief. "How about I pack us some sandwiches and a thermos of coffee?"

"Sounds great," said August. "I'll give you a honk at, let's say, 10:30?"

"I'll be waiting."

Deena turned and started back toward her house. As she walked, she added the slightest extra sway to her hips, just in case August was watching. At one point she chanced a quick look back over her shoulder.

August was looking.

She smiled and waved and then silently thanked God that men – even the most cerebral ones – were so predictable.

* * *

Ramapo was another town in the mountains of North Jersey. But unlike Turtleback Lake, it had no lake to attract outsiders.

Ramapo was set deep in a valley on the far side of a high mountain pass. In the winter, it was often unreachable for days or weeks at a stretch because of treacherous ice and snow. Unless you happened to live there, the town of Ramapo felt remote and godforsaken, almost Appalachian.

Removed from the rest of the world, the inhabitants of Ramapo had an eerie, inbred quality. They were gruff and suspicious toward everybody. But it was on the football field that their native sons showed their truest colors. There they became completely and utterly ruthless and ferocious.

Ramapo High School's mascot was a ram – and not because of the 'ram' in Ramapo. It came from the way that Ramapo players lowered their heads and rammed opposing players with their helmets.

The Rams were throwbacks to an earlier era. They weren't high-fivers or ball-spikers. When they scored a touchdown, they simply dropped the ball to the ground or tossed it to the nearest official. If a player – on their team or the opposition's – had to be carted off, they simply waited for the battle to resume. Football to them wasn't a game – it was a war. Casualties were inevitable. Part of their success came from the fear they instilled in their opponents' minds. But as brutal as they were, there was nothing dirty about them. They simply played harder and tougher than anybody else.

When Deena and August arrived at Turtleback Field, the stands were already packed. They had to climb through the crowd and squeeze into a tiny spot in the top row of the bleachers. They could feel the whole structure flexing under the weight of the stomping sell-out crowd.

Pressed against Deena, August could feel the heat of her body radiating right through his corduroys. Their four thighs, squeezed tightly together, became the tray for their coffee and sandwiches.

The game began. The first quarter was a scoreless defensive battle. The second quarter was more of the same until, with less than a minute left in the half and the Rams driving deep into Snapper territory, Bobby Savarese picked off a pass and raced almost eighty yards for the game's first touchdown.

The crowd stood and cheered wildly. Most remained standing for the extra point attempt. Because of the food on their laps, Deena and August remained seated. They couldn't see JJ Clayton drill the ball through the uprights. But when the crowd roared, August turned to Deena and said, "I guess we made it."

"We certainly did," said Deena with a little smile and wink.

Since their brief summer tryst, August had made no advances toward Deena. He hadn't even flirted with her. She wished he would.

After the extra point, JJ ran off the field. Ian Copeland greeted him on the sideline with a slap on the back.

"Nice kick!" he said.

"Thanks!" said JJ, taking off his helmet.

"Hey – don't you think you should put that back on?" said Ian. He nodded toward the field.

JJ turned around. Everyone on the kickoff team was already out there lining up. Everyone, that is, except for the kicker.

"Yeah – right!" said JJ, pulling his helmet back on and reaching down unconsciously to adjust his cup. "I forgot!"

JJ's kickoff pinned the Rams inside their own 15-yard line. Rather than risk a turnover so deep in their own territory, they took a knee and ran out the clock. Then the two teams headed toward the locker rooms. As the players ran off, the marching band took the field. For the next twenty minutes the blare of brass instruments echoed off the sides of the mountains that surrounded

Turtleback Lake.

In the bleachers, Deena and August stood up and brushed crumbs off their pants. The afternoon was perfect. It was crisp and clear – sweater weather. The night surely would be chilly, down in the high thirties – perfect for curling up in front of a fire. Deena imagined herself snuggling up with August on a rug in front of the fireplace in his cabin – the one with the long-handled ax hanging above it.

"How about some hot chocolate?" August asked her.

"Sure," said Deena, snapped back into the present. "Sounds great."

As they walked from the bleachers to the refreshment stand, dozens of people greeted Deena. Every few steps, somebody new – a student, a parent, or a faculty member – hailed her with a "Good afternoon, Dr. Goode," or "How ya doin', Dr. Goode?" or "Enjoying the game, Dr. Goode?"

And Deena responded to practically each and everyone by introducing them to August.

"Do you know my friend, August Andersen?" she said again and again and again.

The whole thing made August feel awkward. What was everybody going to think – that he and Deena were a couple?

When they finally got on line at the concession stand, August felt a tap on his shoulder. He turned around.

"Long time no see," said Chief Rudolph. "Away on business, Andersen?"

"Just away," said August.

"And now you're back?"

"Back for now."

"Well, August," said Chief Rudolph, "let me be frank. I've been actually kind of hoping that you, because of your special expertise,

might help us here with the unique aquatic problem we're current-
ly experiencing."

"Believe me, Chief," said August. "If I could snap my fingers
and make the problem go away, I would've done it long ago."

"Actually I was hoping you'd try something a little more scientific," said Chief Rudolph. "Unless finger snapping is the best
method you can come up with?"

While August and the Chief were chatting, Deena was at the
concession stand counter, buying two hot chocolates. She turned
around holding a steaming stryrofoam cup in each hand.

"Oh, Chief Rudolph, hi!" she said, handing August his hot
chocolate. "If I had realized you were here – and if I had an extra
hand – I would've gotten one for you, too."

"That's quite all right, Dr. Goode," said The Chief. "But the extra hand I'm actually looking for belongs to your friend, Mr. Andersen."

Suddenly a great rumbling, like a stampede of cattle, shook the
earth beneath their feet. The two teams – eighty football players –
were charging back toward the playing field.

"If I make any headway, I'll let you know," said August.

"I don't mean to interrupt your conversation," said Deena.
"But shouldn't we get back to our seats before we miss any of the
action?"

Chief Rudolph's head shook slowly from side to side as he
watched the two of them walk back toward the bleachers.

* * *

The Rams were set to receive the kickoff to start the second
half.

JJ placed the ball on a tee at the 35-yard line. The players lined up. At top volume, *Start Me Up* by The Rolling Stones blared through the loud speakers. The cheerleaders raised their megaphones and led a cheer that swelled to a roar as JJ's leg swung beneath the ball.

It sailed end over end, deep into Ram territory.

JJ had really nailed it. The ball landed on the five-yard line, took one bounce, and rolled into the end zone. The Rams' deep back picked up the ball and seemed to consider running it out. Then he changed his mind and began lowering his knee to the ground. The onrushing Snappers racing down the field slowed their charge.

It was exactly what The Rams' return man was hoping for.

Just before his knee touched the turf, he took off, sprinting upfield. Fooled by his feint, the Snapper's were a second too slow. He was past them in an instant.

In a flash he was almost to mid-field. And then there was only one player left with a chance of stopping him: JJ.

Coach Lupo had instructed JJ to hang back on all kickoffs – just in case the return man got past the first wave of onrushing defenders. And now it had happened. If JJ didn't tackle him, no one would.

The return man was racing down the left sideline. JJ ran toward him. He thought he had a chance to either tackle him or force him out of bounds. Then suddenly the runner cut back. JJ tried to stop his own momentum by planting his right foot. At the same time he lunged backward in a last ditch effort to trip up the runner. But the cleats on JJ's right shoe stuck in the turf. As he lunged and twisted, searing pain shot up his right leg.

JJ crumpled to the ground. Coach Lupo and Coach Jenkins didn't even wait for the Rams' player to cross the goal line before they started jogging toward their fallen player. JJ was curled up in a ball when they reached him.

JJ looked up through the bars of his facemask.

"I screwed up," he said.

"You didn't screw up," said Coach Lupo. "I did. Don't you worry."

It was the coach's job to prepare his team for any and every eventuality. If they were fooled, he was the fool. It was his fault.

Lupo knelt down on the field.

"Where's it hurt?" he asked.

JJ reached behind his right ankle.

"Did you hear anything snap?" asked Coach Lupo.

"I don't know," said JJ. "Everything was so loud."

Lupo looked up at Jenkins.

"We better play it safe, Georgie," said Coach Lupo. "Get a stretcher. It could be his Achilles."

Coach Lupo turned back to JJ.

"Don't worry, JJ," he said. "This kind of thing can be fixed."

But in his own mind, he was thinking, *But it couldn't be back in the Sixties.*

Back then a torn Achilles was the end. Bill knew. His good friend Oscar knew it, too.

A moment later, a stretcher appeared. Two players and Tufton Mason, the team physician, helped JJ onto it. One of the two players was Ian Copeland.

"Hang in there, JJ," he said. "You're going to be just fine."

As JJ was rolled toward the locker room, he heard a cheer from the bleachers on the visiting team's side. The Rams had made the extra point.

It was the last point scored in regulation time.

In the locker room, Doc Mason gingerly removed JJ's cleats.

"Can you curl your toes up toward your knee?" he asked.

"I'll try," said JJ.

They both looked down at JJ's foot. His toes curled up.

"Good sign," said Doc Mason. "Now try pointing them down – like a ballerina."

JJ did.

"Well," said Doc Mason. "The good new is you didn't tear the tendon. You may have hyper-extended it, but I think you got lucky. You may get away with nothing more than a sprain."

Doc Mason helped JJ get off his uniform and equipment, then he elevated the right foot and wrapped an ice pack around the ankle.

"This will help keep the swelling down," he said. "But your foot's going to be very tender for a number of days."

Doc Mason leaned a pair of crutches up against JJ's locker.

"Until we get the x-ray results, I want you to use these," he said. "I want you to keep all your weight off that foot. Is that clear, JJ?"

"Got it, Doc," said JJ. "And thanks."

* * *

After Doc Mason left, JJ was alone in the locker room. For half an hour he sat icing his ankle, listening to the crowd sounds that came through the open locker room doors. Then everything became quiet. Sixty minutes were up. The game was deadlocked.

The Snappers came clattering into the locker room, their metal cleats scraping and scratching against the tile floor. There was a five-minute break before sudden death began.

Coach Lupo saw JJ with his wrapped ankle. He walked over to him.

"You okay?" he asked, putting a hand on JJ's shoulder.

"Yeah, I'm okay," said JJ.

"You're a lucky kid," said Coach Lupo. "Doc Mason told me it's not your Achilles."

Then he turned to face the rest of the team.

"Listen up, guys," he said. "This is what we've practiced for. This is why we were out here in August busting our guts running wind sprints. This is why we're out on the practice field every afternoon instead of hanging out in a booth down at Bonds'. You guys have gotten yourselves this far. Now it's time to finish what you've started. You gotta reach down inside yourselves for everything you've got left. Are you with me?"

"Yes!" the players shouted. "Yes! Yes! Yes!"

"Then let's go back out there and take what's ours for the taking! Does anybody here wanna be conference champs?"

The players stood and began chanting.

"Snappers! Snappers! Snappers!"

As the players began pulling on their helmets and snapping their chin straps, Bobby Savarese glared through the chipped bars of his facemask. He looked like a wild animal glowering through the bars of a cage. Then he reached down and with the knuckles of both hands he began drumming on the hard enameled shell between his legs. The other players began drumming on theirs. Soon the room was filled with a frenzied hammering of knuckles rapping on the hardened shells of dead snapping turtles.

"Okay, Snappers!" shouted Savarese. "Let's go, go, go, GO!"

The players crowded toward the door then raced back out onto the field.

* * *

The first ten minutes of sudden death was just like the game before it: a defensive battle. Each team went three-and-out, twice. The game went back and forth between the two thirty-yard lines. On the cinder track between the field and the bleachers, the cheerleaders had raised their megaphones and were exhorting the Snapper defense to stiffen.

"Push 'em back, push 'em back, way back!" they chanted for the hundredth time that afternoon.

Mary Robinson was chanting and shaking her pompoms, but her heart was no longer in it. She kept looking back over her shoulder, stealing glances toward the painted metal doors of the boy's brick locker room. They were open.

Suddenly Mary turned to Sandy Danks, the cheerleading captain.

"I've gotta go," she said.

"To the bathroom?" asked Sandy.

"No," said Mary. "I've gotta go and check on something."

Sandy saw Mary steal another look toward the boy's locker room.

"You can't go now, Mary," said Sandy. "You've just got to wait."

"I can't," said Mary. "I've got to go now."

Mary put down her megaphone and pompoms. She ran across the practice field like a gazelle. When she reached the steps to the locker room, she took them two at a time. She ran through the open locker room doors without hesitating.

"JJ?" Mary called out once she was inside. The locker room was an unfamiliar maze of metal lockers and wooden benches.

"Mary?" JJ called back, hardly believing his ears.

Mary came around a corner and saw JJ sitting in front of his locker, his right foot elevated, wrapped, and iced.

"Mary!" he said. "You can't be in here."

Mary ignored him.

"Are you okay?" she asked, sitting down so close that the skin of their bare thighs touched.

"I think I'm going to be fine," said JJ. "Doc Mason says my Achilles isn't torn – maybe just a little hyper-extended."

"Oh, thank goodness!" said Mary. "The way your leg twisted – it made me think the worst. I was really worried."

Mary's gaze suddenly dropped down to JJ's bare torso.

JJ looked down too. The claw marks across his chest and stomach weren't a pretty sight. JJ tried to cover himself with his two hands.

"You don't have to cover yourself," said Mary. "I saw them in the paper."

"I know they're ugly," said JJ. "You're probably disgusted."

"They're not so ugly, JJ," said Mary. "Want to know how I know?"

JJ nodded.

"Because I cut the picture out of the paper," she smiled. "And saved it."

JJ blushed.

For a minute they said nothing. The silence and the wooden benches made it feel like they were in church. It was strange to be alone together when practically everybody else in the whole town was just a hundred yards away.

"I didn't see your father in the stands today," said Mary, breaking the silence.

"I know," said JJ. "He had some kind of real estate thing he had to attend in New York. I told him I didn't mind."

"Oh," said Mary, with a look that said her mind had already

moved on to something else.

Then Mary leaned toward JJ. She began to close her eyes and part her lips. Their lips were about to touch when a loud roar made them both jerk back.

"I think somebody just scored," said JJ.

"Or almost," smiled Mary.

"You better go," said JJ. "You don't want to be in here when the team comes back in."

"All right," said Mary. "If you say so."

Then she began to chant in the softest, singsong voice.

"Hey, ho, twenty-four, watch me walk right through that door!"

Mary bounced up and started skipping toward the door. JJ's eyes were glued to her. Mary looked back once and smiled.

"Caught ya!" she said.

Two minutes later, the cleats of forty players came clattering up the concrete steps into the locker room.

"What happened?" asked JJ, as the team burst in. "Did we win?"

"By a field goal!" shouted Ken Lubowsky. "A fifty yarder!"

"Who kicked it?" asked JJ.

"Copeland did," said Lubowsky. "He limped out there and drilled it through the uprights – with his fake foot."

August explored the lake every morning for two weeks straight. Still he hadn't seen the slightest sign of Grundel.

Wherever the giant snapper was, it was not being lured out of its lair by the strange underwater vessel that was trespassing in its domain.

And still no one – except Deena – knew what August was up to. Chief Rudolph remained in the dark.

Getting into the lake unnoticed was easy. August went out each morning before dawn. It was resurfacing that concerned him. He surfaced as close to shore as possible, and then quickly hid the sub in the undergrowth that grew right down to the shoreline. Still, in those few minutes, there was always the chance that someone would spot him.

It was Connie Konsulis who eventually did.

Since she had been the one who spotted Jack Sully's body, Connie also wanted to be the one who spotted the giant snapper. Each morning she took her morning coffee out onto the deck and scanned the lake below. She was sure that one morning she would look out and there it would be: the domed shell of the giant snapper breaking the surface. Connie even put Chief Rudolph's number on speed dial.

And now as she looked toward the lake's western shore, Connie saw something strange pop up to the surface. It was too far away to say exactly what it was but she wasn't going to wait. She hit Chief Rudolph's number.

"Chief Rudolph here," he answered.

"I can see it now!" Connie said into her cell phone. "It's coming out of the water right this second – over on the far shore!"

"Hold on a second!" said Chief Rudolph. "Who is this? And what's surfacing where?"

"It's me, Chief. Connie Konsulis! It's the snapper! I just saw it surface across the lake from me – near the old Andersen cabin. What should I do?"

Chief Rudolph didn't answer.

He hated to be rude to Connie – her sparkly pink running

shorts were still vivid in his mind – but every second counted.

"Hello!" said Connie. "Chief Rudolph? Are you there? Did I lose you?"

She had lost him. Chief Rudolph was already in the front seat of his cruiser, gravel shooting out from its rear wheels as he sped out of the lot.

* * *

August had just slid his sub into the bushes.

"So that's what you've been up to," said Chief Rudolph.

August looked up. Chief Rudolph was standing there with a shotgun cradled in his arms.

Like Jack Sully, Chief Rudolph was ready to blast the snapper straight to hell. But there was one thing he wanted the beast to leave behind: its shell. Chief Rudolph wanted to hang it above his fireplace. He didn't even mind the idea of bullet holes in it. He imagined himself absent-mindedly fingering the holes as he told the tale of how he had killed the giant snapper in Turtleback Lake.

"I didn't hear you drive up, Chief," said August.

"I turned off the engine and just kind of rolled in," said The Chief. "Quiet-like."

"Well, what can I do for you?" asked August.

"Well, actually, August, I was just wondering if you've seen any of the signs that Deputy Rhodes has gone to such great lengths to post prominently around the perimeter of the lake."

"I've seen them," answered August.

"But have you *read* them?" asked Chief Rudolph. "That's the real question. You know, by law, I could arrest you here and now."

"And what good would that do anyone?" said August.

"Maybe it wouldn't do anyone any good," said Chief Rudolph,

"But it'd be a lot better than having a situation in which maybe your little sub there malfunctions out in the middle of the lake and sinks to the bottom without a trace. Then I've got yet another problem on my hands."

"I've been coming and going around here for years," said August. "If I sank to the bottom, nobody would even notice."

"I'm thinking you're wrong, there, August. I'm thinking that maybe your new next door neighbor might notice."

August remained silent. He had the right to do so.

"All I'm driving at, August – and I'm a reasonable man – is that I'd like to know what you're up to. You can't be in on this thing all by yourself."

Chief Rudolph felt the weight of the double-barreled shotgun resting in his arms. The fingers of his left hand were curled around its cool metal barrels. The fingers of his right hand gripped its smooth wooden stock.

"Well, Chief," said August. "The thing is – judging from the gun you've got in your arms – the two of us seem to want to deal with this problem differently."

"August – just keep me informed. You hear?"

* * *

For weeks, the trees in and around Turtleback Lake had been a blaze of glorious autumnal colors. But now most of the leaves had fallen. They were either plastered to the ground or skittering around in the gusts of late November.

People in Turtleback Lake were relaxed about leaf removal. Most houses were in wooded settings. Homeowners just left their leaves lying where they fell. By spring, they would be gone, reclaimed by the earth. They were just another part of nature's great cycle of life, death, and renewal.

Still, some leaves had to be removed. Like the ones that were clogging the gutters of Dr. Goode's new home. She wondered who could give her a hand. When she saw JJ leaving school on Friday afternoon, she called to him.

"No more football practice?" she asked, already knowing the answer.

"Nope," said JJ. "We're done."

"And how about your foot?" asked Dr. Goode. "Is it getting better?"

"It's pretty good," answered JJ. "I've still got a little limp but Doc Mason says I should be a hundred percent soon."

"I'm happy to hear that," said Dr. Goode.

Then after a pause she added, "Actually, JJ, I was wondering if you might be interested in making a little money over the weekend – now that you've got your Saturdays free."

"Sure," said JJ. "Doing what?"

"Cleaning my gutters," said Dr. Goode. "I don't know whether you know this, but I just bought a bungalow across the lake from you. The gutters are filled with leaves and I could really use somebody to help me get them out."

* * *

The next morning, Judd was already in the kitchen having coffee when JJ came downstairs.

"How about some eggs and bacon, JJ?" asked Judd.

"I can't," said JJ. "I'm late."

"Late?" said Judd. "Late for what? It's Saturday."

"Dr. Goode asked me if I could give her a hand," explained JJ. "I'm going to help clean out the gutters of her new home."

Before Judd could say another word, JJ was out the door. A moment later, he was on his bike and on his way.

That damn woman! thought Judd.

Judd ran through the litany of grievances he had with Dr. Deena Goode. Could one woman have caused one man more torment? And Judd partially blamed himself. If he hadn't recommended Deena to the school board, she would have been long gone. But he had – and now, not only was she the new high school principal, she was also the new owner of a house that he'd been unable to sell! And who knew what was going on between her and that August Andersen? Back in the summer she'd dropped Judd like a hot potato and cozied up to him instead. It would have been better, thought Judd, if she had simply vanished at the end of the summer. What was the old saying? *Out of sight, out of mind.*

And now, thought Judd, as if Deena were sadistically torturing him, *now she's got my son doing chores around her house!*

Judd shook his head. He could hardly believe it. He suddenly realized that he hadn't been simply *thinking* his thoughts in his head like a normal sane person. He'd been saying them aloud – like a deranged lunatic.

The whole damn thing was too damn much.

* * *

JJ did a double-take when he wheeled into the dirt drive in front of Dr. Goode's bungalow. Dr. Goode was out front, wearing black stretch pants and a white tee shirt that clung tightly to her breasts and hung loose at her waist. She looked nothing like the woman in a suit that JJ saw every day at school. Dressed like this, Dr. Goode almost looked like a young woman. JJ thought she actually looked pretty good – for a grownup.

"Would you like some coffee?" asked Deena, gesturing with the cup in her hand. "It's fresh-brewed and hot."

"No thanks," answered JJ. "I'm fine."

"Okay, then," said Deena. "Then why don't we get started. I'm not sure how long this is going to take."

Deena helped JJ lean the ladder up against the side of the house.

"I'll hold the base," said Deena. "While you climb up and scoop out the leaves, okay?"

JJ scrambled up the ladder. Soon, sopping wet clumps of sticks and leaves were plopping to the ground. As he reached out, JJ's shirttails came untucked. Looking up from below, Deena could see the claw marks on the boy's torso. It made her flash back to the summer – when she had raked the flesh on JJ's father's back with her own fingernails. She remembered the red welts they had raised. Judd had moaned and said she was good, very good.

"Not just good," she had thought to herself before her passion passed and a dark mood set in, "Deena Goode."

The wet clumps kept plopping down around her, like cow pads in a field.

Then suddenly somebody startled her.

"I see you've got a helper," said a voice from behind.

Deena spun around, making sure not to let go of the ladder she was holding for JJ.

"Oh, hi," said Deena. "You scared me."

"Sorry," said August.

Deena nodded up toward JJ.

"Do you know JJ?" she asked. "Judd Clayton's son."

August shook his head.

Deena called up to JJ.

"JJ," she said. "I don't know if you've met my neighbor. This is

Mister August Andersen."

"No, I don't think we've ever met," said JJ, calling down from the top of the ladder. "Nice to meet you, Mr. Andersen."

"Nice to meet you, too, son," said August.

As they were introducing themselves, Deena looked back and forth between the two. Suddenly it struck her who JJ looked like – *he looked just like August!* It was strange and inexplicable, but the resemblance was undeniable.

While Deena looked at them, both August and JJ suddenly winced and clutched at their stomachs. Then, eerily, they both turned and looked toward the lake.

Things just weren't happening with August.

After the big game, he had driven Deena home. But when they pulled up in front of her bungalow, August simply thanked her for a nice time and then wished her a good night. Deena's fantasy for the evening – the two of them curled up in front of the fire – went *poof!* She didn't even feel right inviting him over for dinner – so she didn't.

That night, she left the blinds to her bathroom window open. With the trees now bare, August would be able to see her lighted window clearly from his cabin. And if he happened to catch a glimpse of her as she was getting into the shower – or toweling herself dry afterward – what harm was there in that? It might just stoke some embers. As she lathered herself in the shower, Deena had fantasized that August wouldn't even bother to call. He'd stalk through the woods and come to her door like a hungry wolf. She imagined the urgent, insistent banging on her door: let me in, let me in, or I'll blow your house down.

If only, she thought.

But no knocks came that night or in the nights that followed.

Now, a week later, her gutters were clean and her house was shaping up nicely, but it looked like she'd be spending another Saturday night home alone. It seemed as if August's brief morning visit was all she was going to get.

Deena poured herself a glass of wine and curled up in an armchair by the window. She opened a book she'd had for years, but never read: *Jaws* by Peter Benchley. Of course she'd seen the movie, but didn't they always say that the book was usually better? Deena sighed and started to read. If she had to be alone, at least it was a good night for a thriller.

The crisp clear afternoon had given way to a night of howling wind and slashing rain. The boughs of the trees shook like pompoms while the tips of branches scraped, scratched, and knocked against the clapboard sides of Deena's bungalow. Amid the clatter, Deena didn't hear the urgent knocking at her door. But then, as it grew louder and harder, she did. Her heart leapt. She wasn't frightened. She was sure that August had finally come!

Deena tossed *Jaws* aside. The book fell closed to the floor. She didn't care about losing her place. She rose from her chair and went to the mirror in the front hall. She pushed back a lock of wavy black hair that had fallen across her face. Then she reached for the front door's dull brass knob and turned it. Her heart was beating wildly. She pulled the door open.

There, in the cone of light that shone down from the naked bulb above, stood Judd Clayton.

"I know I should've called," he said. "But I knew what you would say."

Judd was dripping wet. It wasn't just raining now – it was pouring. If she asked him in, he'd make a big puddle on the floor. But she felt she had no choice.

"You're completely drenched, Judd," she said. "Come on in."

As Judd stepped through the narrow doorway, Deena could smell his breath.

"You've been drinking, Judd. Did you drive here?"

"No."

"Well, it's a long walk on a night like this."

Judd's clothes were soaked through. The rain outside was now falling in sheets. Somewhere on the far side of the deluge a full moon hid behind a mountain of black clouds.

Deena shook her head at the sight of Judd.

"We're going to have to get you out of those wet things," she said.

Judd started unbuttoning his shirt.

"Whoa, there, partner," said Deena. "You can change in the bathroom."

Deena looked down at the widening puddle on the floor. "You're dripping all over," she said. "Go and get those things off. I'll get you something to change into."

As she looked for something that Judd could wear, Deena thought about August. What if he looked out his window now – and saw a man undressing in her bathroom? It was entirely possible. The blinds were still open. And who knows – maybe it would be good. Maybe it would stir up a little jealousy in August.

Deena knocked on the bathroom door.

"You can put this on while your clothes are drying," she said, handing Judd a white terry cloth robe through the crack in the door.

Judd handed Deena a balled-up wad of dripping wet clothes.

She had to wring them out over the kitchen sink, item by item. Otherwise they'd take forever to dry. Deena wanted to keep Judd's visit as brief as possible. Ever since their summer dalliance, she'd done a good job of keeping him at a distance. She didn't want anything to change now.

"Sit down," she said to Judd, once his clothes were tumbling in the dryer. "Have some coffee."

Judd pulled out a chair and sat down at the kitchen table.

Coffee, he thought. He remembered spying on Deena and August as they put away two bottles of wine in the summer. Wine leads to one thing, he thought, coffee leads to another – *nothing*.

Then again, they had gone to Bonds' for a cup of coffee the day they met.

"Coffee sounds great," said Judd, trying to mask his disappointment.

After she'd poured him a cup, Deena sat down across the table. Judd noted that *she* was having wine.

"You know, Deena, it's not easy being a single dad," said Judd.

"I imagine it's not," said Deena.

When Judd didn't go on, Deena had to say something. "You know, you never told me why your wife left."

"It's a painful subject," said Judd.

"I didn't mean to pry," said Deena.

"No," said Judd. "You're not prying. I want you to know."

Judd took a sip of his coffee. Deena sipped her wine.

"The whole story is this," said Judd. "One day, when JJ was still just a baby in diapers, she left."

"That's it?" said Deena.

"That's it," said Judd. "The whole tragic tale."

"But why?" asked Deena. "Why did she leave?"

"That's what's so painful," said Judd. "I have no idea. She never said. One day she just said, 'I'm sorry, but this can't go on any longer. I'm leaving.'"

"And then what?" asked Deena.

"Then she just left me – me and JJ. She didn't take a thing with her. And she didn't offer a word of explanation. It's been a hard thing to live with."

"But you must have some idea," said Deena. "There had to be something wrong."

"Things had been okay," said Judd. "Or so I thought – until JJ was born. The strange thing was, instead of loving the baby, she seemed almost repelled by him. She didn't want to hold him or change him or feed him. It was like the sight of him filled her with disgust. I couldn't understand it. But if that's the way she felt, I guess it's actually good that she left. But it hasn't been easy."

"I can see why," said Deena. "But you should be proud. JJ's a wonderful boy."

"Thanks," said Judd. "He's been my whole life. But maybe now you can understand. When a woman leaves you like that, it leaves a big hole inside you."

"I do understand," said Deena.

In the silence that followed, Deena heard the clothes in the dryer stop tumbling. They should be dry.

"That's why – this summer," said Judd. "Well, it really meant something to me."

"I'm sorry about that, Judd," said Deena. "I really am. We shouldn't have done what we did – and it's my fault. And then you did me such a favor – helping me get this new job. I feel terrible."

"But why can't we –"

Deena cut Judd off.

"We just can't," said Deena. "There's somebody else I have those kind of feelings for. But I hope we can remain friends."

The word *'friends'* did it.

"Remain friends!" snapped Judd. "When were we ever friends?"

"Well," said Deena. "Maybe I should've said, 'I hope we can become friends.'"

"*Friends?* After what we did together?" said Judd. "I'm sorry, Deena, but I don't think I can stand the downgrade."

Judd rose suddenly. The legs of his chair scraped the wood floor beneath him. He cinched the belt of the terry cloth robe that was doing such a poor job of keeping him decent.

Judd lurched toward the door, stopping only to slip his bare feet back into the topsiders that Deena had propped up against a baseboard heater. They were now stiff, hot, and dry. Judd jerked open the door.

"Judd!" cried Deena. "You can't go out that way. Sit back down and I'll get you your clothes!"

But Judd was like a charging bull. There was no turning back. He stormed through the open door and stomped down the slippery slope toward the lakeshore. His kayak was stowed in the bushes.

Earlier in the night, when he had first set out to cross the lake, Judd had thought of himself as Washington crossing The Delaware. But now the whole thing was a fiasco. *What had he been thinking?* He must have been out of his mind! And now he had to paddle all the way back. Thank God the rain and wind had begun to relent. Judd pushed the kayak off from shore, climbed in, and started paddling.

As the rain slackened, the moon found a hole in the ragged clouds above and began shining through.

At least there'd be moonlight for Judd to see by.

* * *

Far below the lake's choppy, white-capped surface, Grundel was navigating the twisting labyrinth that snaked through the mountain that the world knew only as Turtleback Rock. Grundel's lair was a cavity deep within that underwater mountain. August had come perilously close to discovering it on his first outing. He'd turned around just a bit too soon.

Now, Grundel was feeling a strong stirring in his gut. Something was drawing him out – and he knew what it was. It was his master calling. And Grundel's master was the moon – that not-so-inert rock in the sky that was even now peeking through the clouds at a foolish little man kayaking across the lake.

Judd was a good distance from shore when the wind suddenly picked up again. Moments later fresh torrents of rain began to fall. The moon slipped back behind the clouds. The brief intermission that had lured Judd into a false sense of security was over. Act two had begun.

Judd paddled frantically, but he couldn't control where he was going. He was no longer crossing the lake toward the eastern shore. Now he was being swept swiftly and inexorably southward, toward the once-white rock in the middle of the lake.

Judd cursed himself. What an ass he was! He was a father with a son to care for. But what had he done? He'd drunk too much and acted like a lovesick fool. Now he was going to have to pay the price.

His cries for help were pointless. The howling wind made a mockery of Judd's puny human voice. His desperate cries were drowned out as completely as the lake would soon drown him.

"I'm so sorry, JJ!" he wept.

The tears that coursed down his face, mixed with the cold wet rain, were not about the imminence of his death. They were for failing his son. First the boy had no mother. Now he'd have no dad.

Judd's kayak was now pinwheeling across the lake. First it spun in one direction then it whipped back in the exact opposite. Judd slapped and stabbed at the waves with his paddle, but it was no more use than a teaspoon. Meanwhile the wind and waves battered him like a heavyweight boxer going in for the knockout.

The heavens were against him – and so was hell.

Grundel was now emerging from the mouth of his cave. He sensed something in the water above. He began his ascent.

As he neared the surface, Grundel spotted the hull of a tiny craft just above him. His neck stiffened like a battering ram. He would tear through that hull like it was wet toilet paper.

* * *

Deena had a bad feeling.

Judd's departure was rash and stupid. Was he going to walk all the way home in the wind and rain in a terry cloth robe? Judd was a grown man; he was responsible for his actions, yet Deena couldn't stop thinking that she should be doing something – and doing it before it was too late.

Deena looked at the clock. It was almost midnight. Judd had left over an hour ago. He should be home by now.

Deena opened the directory. Clayton was easy to find. Judd had paid extra to have his name printed in bold-faced capital letters. He didn't want anybody – buyers or sellers – to miss him. Deena dialed the number.

The phone rang five times. Maybe Judd had gotten home and was already asleep. Five rings were enough. Deena was lowering the receiver toward the cradle when she heard a voice.

"Hi! You've reached the Clayton residence. To leave a message for Judd, JJ or Clayton Realty, please begin at the tone."

Voice mail, thought Deena. She waited for the beep.

"Hi. This is Deena – I mean Dr. Goode. Judd, I just wanted to make sure that you got home safely. Please call me as soon as you get this message. Thanks."

Deena hung up the phone but she didn't let go of the receiver. Again she thought of calling August. But what would she even say? She looked out her window toward his cabin. The windows were all dark. He had to be asleep.

She let go of the phone and sat down in a chair. Seconds later she stood back up. She started pacing the floor. Going to bed was out of the question. She looked out her window toward the lake and tried to make out a light in the Clayton house on the far shore. There was no way to see through the pouring rain.

Deena decided to wait until 12:30 for Judd to call back. The minutes ticked away. At 12:25 she went to the hall closet, took out a yellow rain slicker, and put it on. She grabbed the car keys off a hook by the front door and went out into the night. She didn't even bother to lock the door behind her.

The Volvo's headlights strained to illuminate the darkness. The rain was teeming once again. The windshield wipers swiped back and forth like a manic metronome, but they were doing a lousy job. Her defroster was doing a lousy job, too. With one hand still on the wheel, Deena used the other to try to clear a hole in the condensation on the windshield.

Deena followed the snaking curves of Lakeview Drive, heading east around the north end of the lake. She had never been to Judd's house, but she had the address. She had quickly circled it in the directory then torn the whole page out. Now it lay crumpled on the empty seat next to her. 4 Skytop Road. How hard could it be to find?

* * *

The phone hadn't awakened JJ, but the persistent ringing of the doorbell did. He woke with a start and looked at the lighted dial of the clock at his bedside. One o'clock. Who could be at the door at this hour? He gave his father a minute to get it, but when the ringing continued, he threw back the covers, got up, and went down the stairs. He was sure he'd run into his father, bleary eyed, on the way down. But he didn't.

JJ went to the front hall and peered through the glass alongside the door. Dr. Goode, in a yellow slicker with the hood up, was standing, dripping wet, on the welcome mat outside.

JJ opened the door.

"Dr. Goode!" he said. "What are you doing here?"

"I called, JJ," she said. "But no one answered."

"I didn't hear it," said JJ. "And I guess my dad didn't either. We were both asleep."

"Are you sure?"

"Sure of what?" asked JJ.

"That your father's asleep," said Dr. Goode.

"It's one o'clock in the morning," said JJ. "Where else would he be?"

"He came to my house earlier in the evening," explained Dr. Goode. "Did he ever come home?"

"I never knew he went out," said JJ. "I went to bed early."

"You'd better check, JJ. Quick – where's his bedroom?"

"Upstairs," said JJ. "I'll be right back."

JJ took the stairs two at a time. He looked into his father's room. The bed was empty, still made from the previous day.

JJ came back down the stairs, calling through the house.

"Dad! Dad! Are you here?"

There was no answer.

JJ looked out the window.

"But his car's here," he said.

"He told me he didn't drive," said Dr. Goode. "I figured he walked."

"My dad never walks anywhere," said JJ.

"Maybe he took your bike," suggested Dr. Goode.

"That's even less likely."

"Well how else could he have gotten all the way across the lake?" Dr. Goode asked.

JJ went over to the wall and reached for a panel of switches. He flicked two, then slid open the glass doors that led out onto the deck. He walked over to the railing, followed by Deena. They both looked down. Far below, at water's edge, the Claytons' dock was illuminated.

"*Uh-oh!*" said JJ.

"What is it?" asked Dr. Goode.

"My dad's kayak," said JJ. "It's gone."

"Oh my God!" said Dr. Goode. "C'mon!"

"Where are we going?" asked JJ.

"To get help!"

JJ grabbed a windbreaker in the hall closet then the two of them ran out to Deena's Volvo and hopped in. With JJ calling out the lefts and rights, they got back out onto Lakeview Drive in half the time it had taken Deena to find her way in. She handed her cell phone to JJ.

"Try and reach Chief Rudolph," she said.

"What should I tell him?" asked JJ.

"Just get him on the line," said Dr. Goode. "Then give me the phone."

"Where are we going now?" asked JJ.

"To my neighbor's house – Mr. Andersen's. I introduced you this morning."

Deena sped around the north end of the lake. When JJ got Chief Rudolph on the line, he handed the phone back to Deena. She blurted out the situation, never once reducing her speed as she raced along the wet curving roadway.

"Another damn fool," spat out Chief Rudolph. "We seem to be running a surplus."

"So what are you going to do?" demanded Deena.

"I'll take out the patrol boat with Deputy Rhodes," he said. "But don't hold your breath."

Deena hung up.

"What did he say?" asked JJ.

"He said not to worry," she told him. "He said they'll find him."

What was the point in quoting a pessimist?

Turning off Lakeview Drive, Deena careened down the dark dirt road that wound through the woods. She drove past her own bungalow and pulled up in front of August's cabin. She honked the horn of her Volvo. Within seconds a light came on in August's darkened bedroom. By the time Deena and JJ got out of the car and reached the door, August was standing there in his pajamas.

Both Deena and JJ looked wild-eyed.

"What's going on?" asked August.

"I think JJ's dad is out on the lake," said Deena. "We've got to do something."

August looked past the two rain-soaked figures. Behind them he could make out the lake. The surface was a tempest of white-caps.

"What's he doing out there on a night like this?" asked August.

"It's a long story and there's no time to tell it," said Deena. "All I know is there's a good possibility that he's out there right now in a kayak trying to cross the lake."

"Did you notify Chief Rudolph?"

"I just called him," said Deena. "He and Deputy Rhodes are going out in the patrol boat."

August quickly considered the odds of them finding Judd.

"I'll do what I can," said August.

"And what's that?" asked Deena.

"I'll go look for him myself."

"In your little sub?" asked Deena.

"In my little sub," said August. "It's all I've got."

* * *

Judd's kayak crashed against the side of the rock with a bone-crunching thud.

The gale that had swept him so far off course was now beating him like a rug against Turtleback Rock.

Judd was half in and half out of the kayak. From the waist down his body was trapped inside the craft. Each time the waves slammed him against the rock, Judd tried to grasp the slippery surface. Judd knew he had to free himself quickly before he was smashed to smithereens – or else swept back out onto the lake. Either way he'd be a dead man.

Judd Clayton hadn't been to church in years, but still he beseeched the heavens.

"Dear God, please, help me!"

And then the heavens answered. The fingers of Judd's right hand slipped an inch into a narrow fissure in the surface of the rock. In the brief instant he had, Judd pulled with all his might and yanked himself free of the bucking kayak.

The terry cloth belt that had kept Deena's robe closed was long gone. Judd's bare flesh was pressed up against the cold wet rock as he inched himself up the side. Waves pounding against his back tried to drag him back into the churning lake. Judd's flesh was scraped raw and bloody; the surface of Turtleback Rock appeared smooth – until one's naked body was ground against it. When Judd finally clawed his way to the top of the rock, he clung to it for his life. He had no idea he was at the peak of a mighty mountain.

Judd shivered uncontrollably. The wet, white terry cloth robe, twisted around his torso and legs, offered no warmth and little protection. Judd saw himself as if from above: a tiny figure clinging to a rock in a storm-tossed sea. He thought of *The White Rock Girl* imprinted on soda bottles when he was a kid. She had been perched on a rock like this. Only she had had wings on her back – like an angel. She could fly away. He couldn't. He wondered how much longer he could hold on before some wave knocked him back into the freezing water.

* * *

"I'm coming with you," said JJ. "It's my father out there!"

August had dragged the sub out of the bushes and into the water. Waves were crashing like breakers against the shore. August gripped the rungs on the side of the craft, trying to steady it so he could climb in.

"You can't come," he said to JJ. "There's no room for you."

"It's a two-seater," argued JJ.

"You're right, JJ," said August. "And that second seat is where your father's going when I find him."

August had gotten himself on top of the rocking sub and was lowering himself into the hatch. He called back to JJ.

"Stay here with Dr. Goode. Your dad and I will need you both when we get back."

Then August closed the hatch. The sub motored off shore, listing wildly from side to side in the turbulent waters. In the renewed downpour, it was underwater even before it submerged. Within seconds, JJ and Dr. Goode lost all sight of it.

"There's nothing we can do now but wait," said Dr. Goode. "Come on, JJ, let's get inside."

They went inside August's cabin and took up position by the window where Deena had spent her summer writing. They looked toward the lake, peering through the rain and darkness, but they couldn't make out a thing.

Out there, somewhere, Chief Rudolph and Deputy Rhodes were braving the storm. The Chief clung to the boat's steering wheel, straining to see through the rain-streaked windscreen. At the same time he was trying to recall who played the skipper on *Gilligan's Island*. The guy kind of looked like Rod Steiger, but it wasn't him. It was a stupid thing to be thinking of but it had come to him because of the show's theme song: *The weather started getting rough, the tiny ship was tossed.* It was *apropos*.

Meanwhile, Deputy Rhodes called out through a bullhorn: "Judd! Judd Clayton! Judd – are you out there?"

Chief Rudolph and Deputy Rhodes had motored across the lake from the town basin at the south end. Now they were in the north end, where they assumed Judd was most likely to be found – somewhere between the Burt bungalow on the western shore and the Clayton house on the east side.

Though Chief Rudolph's approach made perfect sense, August had taken a different tack. Despite long years of scientific training,

August was letting himself be guided by his gut. And his gut was sending him straight out into the middle of the lake.

August was bound for Turtleback Rock.

* * *

Wind and waves weren't the only forces pummeling Judd's kayak against the side of Turtleback Rock.

Rising from below like a torpedo, Grundel rammed the kayak's hull with his razor-sharp beak, punching out a hole as big as his head. The tasty legs and crunchy feet he expected inside weren't there, so he rammed the kayak again and again, poking two more gaping holes into its hull. Grundel was like a giant woodpecker, drilling for food.

Judd was now splayed like a starfish across the top of the rock. He watched his kayak in the water, jerking and lurching spasmodically. It now seemed out-of-sync with the waves that were thrashing it. Judd didn't know that Grundel was ravaging his kayak from below.

And Grundel was very angry. The moon had summoned him to a feast. And now there was nothing in the little boat for him to eat. Grundel opened his jaw wide and gripped the kayak's hull. Then he dragged the whole damn thing underwater.

Wow, thought Judd. *That went down fast.*

* * *

Suddenly, from out of the rain-slashed darkness, a beam of light struck Judd. It shone on him for just an instant, lighting up his blood-streaked body. Then the beam was gone, illuminating nothing but slanting sheets of pouring rain.

Plunged back into darkness, Judd lifted his head and cried. "I'm here!" he shouted. "I'm here!"

He couldn't believe that a rescue team had been sent out – and that it had found him.

August had seen Judd, but holding the sub steady on the choppy surface was impossible. August couldn't keep the beams of his headlamps trained on anything for more than a second.

At least August knew he had come to the right place. But now the waves that had pounded Judd's kayak against the rock were doing the same to his sub. Each time it banged against the rock, it clanged like a channel gong. Inside the sub, August was being thrown about from side to side.

There was no way for August to steady it. He'd just have to do the best he could under the worst possible conditions.

"Here goes nothing," he said, unlatching the hatch. When he stood, he gripped the rim of the hatch with one hand, while extending the other toward Judd.

"Give me your hand!" he shouted.

Judd began inching toward August's outstretched hand. The sides of the rock were sloped and slippery. One false move and Judd could slide right back into the water. And the sub was banging against the rock with loud metallic clangs. If Judd lost his grip, he could easily get crushed between the sub and the rock.

"Keep coming!" August shouted.

Judd kept inching down, trembling from cold and fear. But the closer he came to August's hand, the steeper the sides were pitched. Suddenly, he began to slide. There was nothing to stop him. As his lower body plunged down into the lake, his arms shot up. August reached out, gripping Judd's wrist like a vise. From the neck down, Judd was in the water, and August was hanging far out over the side of the sub.

A sudden wave slammed the sub against the rock. Judd's body was caught between. He cried out. Bones inside him cracked and broke. But still, August's grip held. He didn't let go. And now, with strength he didn't know he had, he began hauling Judd up the side of the sub.

Judd tried to find toeholds for his feet. There were rivets, rungs, and recesses. Ignoring his pain, Judd scrambled up the side of the sub as fast as he could. He knew that at any second he might be crushed again between the sub and the rock. All the while, August gripped his wrist and pulled, dragging Judd toward the open hatch. Judd was now draped like a wet towel across the side of the sub.

"Climb in!" cried August.

"I can't!" said Judd. "I can't go any further."

"Oh God!" thought August. "Here goes."

August hoisted himself out of the sub and climbed down alongside Judd. Clutching a rung with one hand, August got his shoulder under Judd's body and pushed. Judd slid upwards onto the top of the sub. When his body was halfway into the hatch, he fell forward headfirst. August peered down into the hatch. Judd was upside down and bloody, but he was in.

With Judd safely inside, August began climbing back in himself. But then the sub lurched violently. August slipped. He was in the lake up to his neck, but his hand snagged hold of a handle as he fell. He'd have to pull himself up.

"Here goes nothing," he said.

And then, his brain flashed bright white with searing pain from his right leg. But it didn't matter. He still had to pull himself up – and he did. With his left foot, August found a toehold. He pulled up his right leg. He looked down, fearing there would be no foot at the end of it. But there was.

The craft had lurched just as Grundel's jaw snapped shut. He had missed his mark by a fraction of an inch and a tenth of a second.

August climbed into the hatch. Blood streamed from a gash across the back of his right calf. It splattered onto Judd. Though almost unconscious, Judd knew it wasn't rain or lake water. It was too warm and had too much body.

August closed the hatch and secured the clasps. In the seat next to him, Judd Clayton was slumped and curled. It was too much to ask him to sit up straight. With his left foot, August pressed the throttle. Somehow the engine had stayed on. The sub moved away from the rock. August dipped the craft's nose and the sub slid under the surface.

Twenty feet down, the water was strangely calm and unperturbed. It was as though no storm existed here. August peered into the liquid blackness – only one headlamp had survived the pummeling against Turtleback Rock – then he reached over and grabbed a wad of the drenched robe plastered to Judd's back. He let go of the steering wheel and then, with two hands, he tore off a long strip of terry cloth. He wrapped it around his right leg just below the knee then started twisting the two ends round and round, like someone turning off a valve. The flow of blood from the gash above his ankle slowed to a trickle. It had been more than forty years since August's father had taught him how to tie a tourniquet.

"You never know when you'll need one," he had told August. "I've seen them come in handy myself."

* * *

Like a raging beast calmed by a powerful tranquilizer, the storm abruptly died down. Everything became strangely calm.

Within minutes, the surface of the lake became eerily still and flat. From up in the sky, the moon looked down into the valley like a government official called in to assess the extent of the damage.

When the rain stopped, JJ and Dr. Goode stepped outside the cabin. They walked down to the edge of the lake. The low rumble of a motor began to drown out the sound of water lapping against the shore. Soon a bright beam shone across the surface.

"It's Chief Rudolph!" JJ said to Dr. Goode.

They waited till the boat was within shouting distance.

"Did you find my dad?" JJ cried out.

Chief Rudolph was slow to answer. Saying 'no' wasn't always so easy.

"Not yet, JJ," he called back. "But now that the storm's subsided, maybe we'll have better luck."

JJ felt sick to his stomach.

Dr. Goode put an arm around his shoulders.

"There's still hope, JJ," she said.

Then, suddenly, a curved shell began to break the surface. Deena saw it first. "Look out, Chief!" she cried.

Chief Rudolph spun and reached for his rifle. He quickly shouldered it and was taking aim when JJ shouted, "Stop! Don't shoot – it's the sub!"

The sub had popped up like a fisherman's bobber, its curved metal surface glinting in the moonlight. Its one remaining headlamp threw a weak path of light across the water.

On land and on the lake, nobody spoke. They waited in silence for the hatch to open. Twenty, thirty seconds passed. JJ couldn't bear it.

"Something's wrong!" he cried. "Do something, Chief!"

Chief Rudolph piloted his boat closer to the pulverized vessel. The bobbing sub looked like an oversized beer can that Jack Sully might have crushed in his fist before tossing overboard. Deputy Rhodes aimed a flashlight through the sub's windshield.

"They're both in there!" he cried.

"Both?" said Chief Rudolph.

"Andersen and Clayton," said Rhodes. "But they look in pretty bad shape."

Chief Rudolph positioned the police boat right alongside the sub. Deputy Rhodes climbed down and straddled the sub's curved top. He rapped on the windshield. The two men inside didn't respond.

"Release the latch!" shouted Rhodes, hammering on the glass panel with his fist.

August looked up, dazed. Just raising his arms required strength he wasn't sure he had. He fumbled with the latch above his head. Suddenly, the hatch cracked open. Deputy Rhodes reached down and swung it wide. He looked at the two men crammed in the space below.

"*Jeezus*, Andersen – what happened?"

August was sitting in a pool of red that sloshed up past his ankles. If it had all been blood, August would've been dead. But it wasn't. It was a mix – of blood, lake, and rain.

"Chief!" said Deputy Rhodes. "We're going to need an ambulance!"

Deputy Rhodes looked at August again. The expression on his face had changed. Suddenly, August looked completely alert – and alarmed.

"He's coming!" he said.

"Who's coming?" asked Rhodes.

"The snapper," said August.

"How do you know?"

"I can feel it," said August. "In my gut."

"Just calm down now, August. You're probably just in shock."

"I'm not in shock!" cried August. "I'm telling you, it's coming – fast. For God's sake, Rhodes, we've got to –"

* * *

Grundel had followed the strange metal tube with the spinning pinwheel on its tail. He had felt the vibrations it made as it bore through the water. Grundel had lagged well behind, lurking in the wake of bubbles that trailed behind the thing. Grundel did not want to be seen by the thing's one shining eye.

The thing was not small, and on either side it had long barbed prongs that looked formidable. Grundel would be patient. Inside the thing were men whose arms and legs were meant for him.

Grundel watched the thing rise to the surface. Now it was bobbing above him, as oblivious as a duck. Another boat, making even louder vibrations, pulled alongside the tube. He heard the voices of men. The moon had called him out for something special after all. He was going to have a field day.

Grundel poked his head above the surface. There were too many shining lights – they bothered his sensitive yellow eyes. He moved back into the shadows of the floating tube. He looked up. A man in a uniform was straddling the tube.

Grundel looked around. He saw two handles he could reach. He paddled in closer and then, with his right claw, he reached up and grabbed one handle. Then with his left claw, he grabbed the other. Then Grundel did a pull up. The whole metal cylinder rolled toward him. For a brief instant, the eyes of the man straddling the tube looked into Grundel's. Then he slipped from his mount and fell into the water with a muffled cry.

The frigid water was a shock. For a second or two, Deputy

Rhodes was too stunned to do anything. In the water below, Grundel circled languidly. He wanted to strike at just the right angle. How you came in was key.

Deputy Rhodes had to make a quick decision. Try to climb back up onto the sub – or swim to shore.

When he was a teenager, Donnie Rhodes had been on the Turtleback Lake swim team. But that had been twenty-five years ago. Without time to think, Donnie unconsciously assumed that he could still swim now as he had then. He started swimming. It was only forty yards to shore. Back in his prime he could do that in – what – fifteen, twenty seconds? But Donnie wasn't in his prime and he wasn't in a Speedo. He was out-of-shape and he was weighed down with wet clothes and boots.

Still, wet clothes and all, he was now more than halfway to shore. Just another fifteen, twenty yards. But this wasn't a race Deputy Rhodes was going to win – even if he'd still been in his prime. Deputy Rhodes was racing Grundel. And Grundel was going to win.

Dr. Goode screamed, "Hurry – he's right behind you!"

Chief Rudolph raised his rifle, a *.30-30* Winchester, to his shoulder. He aimed at the water just behind his partner. He waited, patiently tracking Rhodes's progress. Grundel was right behind him, just beneath the lake's surface.

Seeing land so close, Deputy Rhodes gave in to another misguided instinct. He stopped swimming and reached for the bottom of the lake with his feet. From here, he thought, it would be faster to run. It was another mistake. Donny's first step slipped on the lake's slippery bottom. Rhodes floundered. Now he was all Grundel's. The great snapper opened his jaw wide. He would take the man's leg just below the thigh. He tilted his body for a better angle. As the edge of his shell broke the surface, Chief Rudolph squeezed the trigger. The echo of the blast, caroming through the valley, made the one shot sound like five or six.

Grundel's jaw snapped shut like a trap as the bullet bore through his shell. His armor slowed the bullet, but it couldn't stop it. Fired from such close range, the bullet penetrated deep into Grundel's body. Grundel banked sharply to the left, seeking the refuge of deeper water. Chief Rudolph saw him clearly. He took aim and fired again. More blasts resounded through the valley.

Chief Rudolph thought his second shot hit the snapper squarely in the back, but he was wrong. The second bullet merely grazed Grundel's shell. Then, after skimming across the lake's dark surface, it started to sink to the bottom. As it sank, the bullet was swallowed in a single gulp by a ravenous pickerel attracted by the allure of its shiny surface.

Deputy Rhodes scrambled onto shore, dripping, gasping and shivering. JJ and Dr. Goode helped him to his feet as an ambulance screeched to a halt in the clearing by the cabin.

Paramedics ran down the slope toward Deputy Rhodes.

"I'm OK," said Deputy Rhodes, as they wrapped a blanket around him. "It's the guys in the sub who need help!"

The beams from the ambulance's headlights lit up the whole scene: Chief Rudolph lowering the Winchester from his shoulder, the sub bobbing alongside the police boat, and the blood red waters that Grundel had left in his wake.

Chief Rudolph looped a line onto the deck of the sub. He flung the other end to JJ and the paramedics on shore. In just minutes, the sub was out of the water and up on land. The paramedics lifted the two men out and quickly laid them on stretchers.

JJ walked alongside the stretcher as the paramedics carried his father to the ambulance.

"Dad!" he cried again and again. "Can you hear me? Dad – it's me – JJ!"

Just as they were sliding him into the back of the ambulance, Judd's eyes opened briefly. He reached out for JJ's hand and squeezed it weakly.

"I love you, JJ," he said in a faint voice. "Please – forgive me."

"There's nothing to forgive, Dad," said JJ. "And I love you, too."

Chief Rudolph stuck his head into the back of the ambulance.

August's head was raised slightly, propped up on a small pillow.

"Did you get him, Chief?" he asked.

Chief Rudolph looked into Andersen's eyes.

"I did, August. I hit him twice – square in the back. He swam off, but there's no way he can survive."

August was silent.

"I know how you feel, August," said the Chief. "But it was either the snapper or Donnie. What would you have done?"

"Exactly what you did," said August.

Paul Murphy, one of the paramedics on duty that night, interrupted their conversation.

"You can talk to them, later, Chief," he said. "But right now, we got to get them to the emergency room."

Paul closed the ambulance's double doors and the vehicle pulled away.

The storm kept Marc up well past midnight. His apartment had a leaky roof. The rain dripped into a small bucket that Marc had to empty every twenty minutes. When the garage doors of the Turtleback Lake Rescue Squad opened suddenly just before 2 a.m., Marc was standing at his window. He watched the ambulance speed out into the night. Throwing a coat over his pajamas, Marc dashed outside and hopped into his own champagne-colored Suburu. He tailed the ambulance all the way to the northwest corner of the lake where it stopped in front of August Andersen's cabin. Marc smelled a story in the making – and he got it.

CHIEF BLASTS SNAPPER!
By Marc Bozian

The residents of Turtleback Lake can heave a collective sigh of relief. The scourge that has terrorized the town has ended.

On Thursday night, at approximately 2 a.m., Police Chief Rudolph fired a bullet that pierced the shell of a giant snapper that was about to add Deputy Donald Rhodes to its list of victims. Donald Rhodes, 42, had fallen into the lake in the midst of a rescue attempt.

According to eyewitnesses, including Dr. Deena Goode, Principal of Turtleback High School, and Judd Clayton, Jr., a freshman at Turtleback High, the turtle was on the verge of attacking Deputy Rhodes when a bullet fired by Police Chief Rudolph struck and splintered the monstrous snapper's shell. The two eyewitnesses concurred that the wounded turtle then fled, billowing great plumes of blood. A second round, fired as the wounded reptile sought the refuge of the deep, added the final nail to the great beast's coffin.

Rudolph and Rhodes were out on the lake, along with August Andersen, in an attempt to rescue Mr. Judd Clayton, the prominent local real estate broker. Mr. Clayton was apparently attempting to cross the lake in a kayak during the raging storm that battered the region that night.

The heroic efforts of Mr. Andersen in particular can be credited for saving Mr. Clayton's life.

Operating a two-man submersible vessel that he helped to design and build, Mr. Andersen rescued Mr. Clayton from Turtleback Rock, where the broker had been stranded when violent waves crashed his kayak against the rock.

What induced Mr. Clayton to risk life and limb on such a reckless, ill-considered crossing has not yet been made clear. Mr. Clayton has been only semi-conscious since the accident, though doctors, who say his condition remains guarded, believe he will make a full recovery from the various injuries he sustained.

* * *

"Some story, Marc," said Michael Schneiderman as the two colleagues were having coffee in a booth at Bonds'.

"Thanks, Mike. All in a day's work."

"You know, you've gotten a lot of mileage out of this snapper," said Michael. "What are we gonna do now – now that the turtle's gone?"

Secretly, Michael was concerned that his new star reporter might be thinking about jumping ship. A few days earlier, when Michael was walking past Bonds', he had glanced through the window and seen Marc talking with some guy who looked a lot like Stephen Borg, the publisher of *The Record*.

"Actually," said Bozian. "I've been approached about a possible book deal."

Schneiderman shook his head in amazement. It was unbelievable! Did absolutely *everything* have to be turned into a book?

"Well, good luck with that," said Michael. "You'll sign me a copy when it's done, okay?"

"I'll do better than that," said Marc. "I'll work you into the story."

"Great," said Mike. "Maybe I can even play myself in the movie."

"I wouldn't joke, Mike," said Marc. "There's been interest."

"So what does all this mean for the paper?" asked Michael.

"It means I'm going to need some time off," said Marc. "Maybe just a few months to work on the book. Then we can see where we stand."

"Well, then," said Michael, spinning and rising off his stool. "I guess this is good bye and good luck for now."

Michael reached out for Marc's hand. It was odd, but the two men had never shaken hands before. As their hands clasped, Marc felt something he had never noticed before: Michael's middle finger ended at the knuckle.

"You know, Mike," he said. "I was just wondering – did you happen to play football here in town when you were in high school?"

Chapter 25

Turtleback Lake December 2006

AFTER THE LONGEST, HOTTEST SUMMER in memory, December turned out to be the polar opposite. An arctic air mass set in and refused to budge. For a week the temperature didn't rise above single digits. Never had the lake frozen so solid so early.

August sat in an armchair, gazing out the window at the skaters gliding and falling out on the lake. His injured foot was elevated and resting on a pillow. He was sipping hot chocolate from a mug. Deena stood behind him, wearing a black cashmere cardigan with mother-of-pearl buttons. August leaned his head back against the soft swell of her stomach. For someone so toned, the curve of her belly was a bit of a surprise. But so what if Deena had suddenly put on a few? What did it matter?

The scene on the lake reminded Deena of a nineteenth-century print that had hung on the wall of her kitchen when she was a little girl.

"It's like a scene from *Currier and Ives*," she said.

"Or perhaps a *Breughel*," suggested August.

This was what Deena loved about August. He understood her. And she understood him.

Deena looked beyond the skaters. In the distance, far across the lake, a solitary figure sat in a folding chair, fishing through a hole in the ice.

"Does anyone ever catch anything ice-fishing?" she asked.

"They must," said August. "Otherwise, why would they do it?"

Given a choice, Deena thought she'd much rather skate and generate body heat than sit freezing by a hole hoping for a fish to come along.

Since the night of his injury, Deena had been faithfully nursing August back to health. He had put in for a leave of absence at the university until he was back on his two feet again. Deena couldn't have been happier. Every day after school, she stopped in at her bungalow, changed into something comfortable, then walked over to August's cabin with a bag of groceries. While she prepared dinner, the two of them sipped wine and talked.

One Friday night, after she had cleared the dishes from the table, Deena was putting her coat on to leave.

"If you feel like it," said August, "why don't you stay?"

Deena sighed and smiled.

"You know," she said. "I was beginning to think you'd never ask."

* * *

It was a frigid starry night, but at least there was no wind.

Five people sat around a fire in a clearing down by the lake. Their faces glowed in the light of the flickering flames. The smoke from the fire rose straight up in a column into the star-filled sky above. The people sat on stools that all had been made from the same tree trunk.

Judd Clayton poured a single-malt whisky into August's mug. It was poured from a bottle he had kept in his liquor cabinet for more than a decade. He had been saving it for a special occasion, but no occasion special enough had ever cropped up. Earlier in the day, when Deena called to invite him and JJ to 'join them around the fire,' Judd decided the right moment finally had come.

"There's something I'd like to say," said Judd, lifting his glass toward the others. "It's not so much a toast as it is a thank-you – and an apology."

Everyone – August, Deena, JJ and Mary – waited for him to continue.

"August, I'd like to thank you for saving my life. I wouldn't be sitting here today if it weren't for you."

August said nothing, but raised his mug in acknowledgement. The two men's eyes met.

Then Judd looked toward Deena.

"I'd also like to apologize for my stupid behavior," said Judd. "I'm truly sorry. I was a total ass. I lost control of myself and my emotions."

"Forget it, Judd," said Deena. "We're all human."

Judd reached out with his mug. August touched his to it. Then they both took a swig. The whisky coursed through the two men, warming them both from within.

On the two stools at the end of the semi-circle, JJ and Mary clinked their mugs together. The hot chocolate they had brought in a thermos was still steaming. After their first sip, Mary reached over and wiped the froth off JJ's upper lip with the knuckle of her index finger.

"You look nice in a mustache," she said. "But even better without."

JJ reached over and wiped the foam off Mary's upper lip.

"You too," he laughed.

Deena rose from her stool.

"I think the fire could use another log," she said.

"Let me," said JJ, starting to rise.

Deena gestured for him to stay seated.

"Thanks, JJ, but actually I kind of like doing it myself."

Deena chose a log from the stack at the edge of the clearing, balanced it on end then raised an ax high above her head. It was the ax August always kept razor-sharp above his fireplace. The ax head fell and split the log neatly in two.

"One swing," said Judd. "I'm impressed."

"I'm getting the hang of it," said Deena. "It's fun."

She tossed the two halves into the fire. A spray of embers flared into the air then rained back down like a shower of shooting stars. In the sudden glow, August glanced across the fire at JJ. He thought the boy had just winced. Then he noticed JJ reaching for his stomach.

"Is something wrong, JJ?" asked August.

"No," said JJ. "It's nothing. Sometimes I just get little twinges in my scar. It's nothing."

Mary wrapped her arm around JJ's shoulder. They leaned closer together. It felt good. But the pain in his scar didn't stop.

August looked again into JJ's eyes. It was weird – too weird to be nothing – but August also had just felt a strange pang in his stomach.

He looked again into the boy's eyes. Something was wrong – and getting worse.

"Want another?"

"You have to ask?"

Ted Tanner handed a cold can of beer to Bobby Savarese. He felt no guilt about drinking with a minor. The kid had stayed back once, maybe even twice, in grade school. Savarese wasn't a kid. He was nineteen – practically twenty. There was nothing wrong with throwing back at few. In some states, he'd already be legal.

"At eighteen it used to be legal in this state," said Tanner.

"What?" said Savarese, not following the line of Ted Tanner's unspoken thoughts.

"Nothing," said Tanner. "Just the drinking age. It used to be eighteen here in New Jersey."

The two men sat on folding stools, sharing a six-pack. They were fishing through a hole they had chipped and sawn through the ice earlier in the night. A gas lantern cast a ring of flickering light. Each man had a fishing pole in one hand and a beer can in the other. Between slurps and burps, they talked.

"Ever catch anything this way?" asked Savarese.

"Nope," answered Ted. "But others have."

"Like who?" asked Savarese.

"The Eskimos."

"This ain't Alaska," said Savarese. "And we're not Eskimos. How about somebody around here?"

"Bill Lupo says he's had luck ice-fishing."

Savarese drained his beer and tossed the empty can into the hole they were fishing in. It bobbed in the freezing water along with other cans they'd tossed in earlier. The cans made Savarese think of the passengers on the *Titanic* – the ones freezing in the water hoping to be saved.

Suddenly the tip of Savarese's pole plunged like a divining rod. When he tried lifting it back up, he couldn't.

"I've got something!" he said. "Something big."

"Let me give you a hand," said Ted.

The two men struggled together.

"The thing weighs a ton!" said Savarese.

"Watch the hole," said Tanner. "You're too close. You'll slide right in."

The two men dug their heels into the ice, but whatever was at the other end of the line kept pulling them closer to the edge of the hole. Tanner and Savarese looked like the losing team in a tug of war.

"Let go of the pole!" shouted Ted.

But Savarese didn't like losing – or quitting. He held on after Tanner let go. Then his feet slid out from under him. A second later, he slid over the edge and into the hole.

"Help!" he cried as he plunged into the water.

The water was freezing – or just a degree or two above. If Ted couldn't get Savarese out quickly, he'd be dead of hypothermia within minutes.

Tanner dropped to his knees and spread himself flat on the ice. He extended his arm. "Give me your hand!" he cried.

Savarese reached to grab it. Tanner felt Bobby's cold wet fingers tightening around his wrist. *Thank God*, he thought – the kid was going to be okay. He'd be able to save him. And then, with a jerk from below, Bobby's fingers let go and he was gone. His head went under like a boulder dropped into the water. The only thing left on the surface was empty beer cans.

"Bobby! For chrissakes!" cried Tanner. "Where are you?"

Ted stood up, grabbed the lantern, and bent over the hole.

"Oh my God!"

In the light of the lantern, Ted could see the water had turned from black to red. As he bent down for a closer look, Grundel's head burst through the surface. Grundel reached up and grabbed Tanner's right ankle. His claws ripped through Tanner's pants, socks, and skin. Grundel yanked.

Ted went down hard. The side of his head banged against the ice. He moaned once and tried to clutch the ice. His fingertips slid across the cold slippery surface as Grundel dragged his body into the water.

A minute later, Grundel's head popped up again. He pulled himself halfway out of the water and then rested with his elbows at the edge of the ice. Beer cans bumped up against his shell. Grundel looked out across the dark lake. Suddenly it began to glow a gorgeous bluish-white. Grundel looked up at the sky. His master's beatific stone face was smiling down.

Grundel craned his neck, surveying the western shoreline from south to north. There were lighted windows in houses all along the shore. Then he spotted a light that was different – a light that flickered and flashed. Somebody was having a campfire up in the northwest corner of the lake. Grundel had visited a campfire there once before. It had been a long, long time ago.

Grundel clambered out onto the frozen lake. Just as he began crawling across the ice, a bluish white head with chattering teeth popped back up to the surface in the hole behind him. The head was Ted Tanner's. Ted was missing an arm now, but he reached up with the one hand he had left – the one with four and a half fingers. He tried to grab the ice, he clawed at it desperately, but it was impossible. Then he slipped back under.

JJ tried to ignore the pain, but he couldn't. He was practically doubled-over.

"What's wrong, JJ?" asked Judd.

"I don't know, Dad. My scar's hurting like never before."

"Let me see," said Judd.

JJ unzipped his coat and lifted up his heavy wool sweater. He was wearing a white cotton tee shirt underneath it. It was streaked with bright red bands of blood.

"JJ!" cried his dad. "You're bleeding!"

"I don't know what's happening," said JJ.

He peeled up the bloody tee shirt. Grundel's claw marks looked as raw and bloody as the night of the attack.

August was also feeling intense pangs.

"Let's all go up the cabin," he said. "As quickly as possible."

"Why?" asked Judd. "What's wrong? What's going on?"

"I'll tell you when we're all safe inside."

"Safe?" said Deena. "Safe from what?"

August looked around. Everybody was staring at him.

"I'm thinking Chief Rudolph was wrong," he said. "I don't think he killed the snapper. I think it's alive – and I think it's coming this way."

"But the lake's frozen solid," said Mary.

"Solid or not," said August, "I think he's coming. Now let's get going!"

The pain from Judd's broken ribs was still excruciating whenever he moved too quickly or suddenly. Running was impossible. Mary took his arm and helped him walk slowly up the slope toward August's cabin. JJ, still bent in pain, walked alongside.

Deena turned to August.

"Should we put out the fire?" she asked.

"Forget the fire," said August. "Just go up to the cabin. I'll meet you there in a minute."

"What do you mean – 'in a minute?'" said Deena. "What are you going to do?"

"I need to get something," said August.

"What?"

"Look, Deena, there's no time for this. Please – just go up to the cabin."

"I'm not going without you."

Deena was adamant and there was no time for arguing. August turned and limped down toward the bushes where his sub was draped with heavy tarps. He started lifting and dragging them aside.

"You're not thinking of going out there?" said Deena. "It's frozen solid."

"No," said August. "I just need one of these."

August started struggling to free one of the spear guns that were mounted to the sides of the sub. Their tips had been treated with a potent tranquilizer that August had hoped – back when he was still searching for the giant snapper – would render his quarry unconscious.

August cursed. Deena was surprised. She had never heard him utter a single expletive – not even a 'damn.'

"What's wrong?" she asked.

"The clasps are frozen – jammed. They won't budge!"

"What can I do?" asked Deena.

"I need something to knock them loose with. Something hard. Something metal."

An idea came to Deena instantly. The ax! She spun around,

took one step then stopped in her tracks.

"August!" she screamed.

August spun around.

Grundel was no more than ten feet away. After crossing the lake, he had crept across the frozen ground behind them. He was between them and the cabin. There was no escape. They were trapped. Deena inched backward till she was pressed up against the sub next to August.

Grundel looked at the two people backed up against the metal tube that had caused him such problems just weeks before. He eyed them balefully. The he opened his mouth and hissed. No steam came out. Grundel was as cold on the inside as the air around him.

He fixed his eyes on August. Him he had already tasted. The little nip he had taken had been quite savory. The flavor had been hauntingly familiar – almost ancestral. But today he would start with the flesh of the quivering woman. She was goose-bumped with terror. This was good. People always tasted better when they were frightened. Fear released something tasty into their blood-streams.

Yes, yes, yes, thought Grundel, looking into the woman's dark brown eyes. *So pretty, so plump, so doomed.*

Grundel crept forward slowly, relishing the terror that kept the woman frozen in place. He began mentally enumerating the savory sensations that awaited him: the mouth-watering meat, the crisp crunch of gristle and bone, the warm salty gravy of blood.

The woman's eyes were fixed on his – mesmerized. She was under his spell. But then, suddenly, she looked away – at something above or behind him. Grundel craned his neck to see what it could possibly be. He turned just in time to see a wedge of steel swishing through the air. It crashed into his shell, splitting his cara-pace like a coconut. Grundel couldn't believe it. It was that same damn ax! There was no mistaking it. He had carried it in his back too long to ever forget. And now it was back – *in his back!* Only this time, it went in deep. The damn blade had hit the fault line it had created eighty years earlier.

Grundel's brain filled with pain. But he kept his head. He knew whoever swung the ax would want to swing it again. Big mistake! People thought they got three strikes. With him, they only got one. Grundel would get this ax-swinger – just as he had gotten the other one long ago.

"Let go of the ax, JJ!" screamed August. "Run!"

Startled by August's cry, JJ let go of the smooth wooden handle. He turned and did exactly what August had told him to do: he ran.

August grabbed Deena's hand and yanked her past the giant turtle. They raced up the slope toward the cabin door. For a man with a limp, August moved pretty quickly.

Grundel looked over his shoulder. There it was: the ax handle – sticking out of his shell like a shovel left behind by a sloppy gravedigger. *These people!* Now he had *two* pieces of steel wedged in him: a bullet and an ax. The first had been bad enough – this second one hurt like hell. There would be no juicy, terror-seasoned flesh for Grundel tonight.

Grundel felt the trickle of blood dripping down through his plastron. He looked down at the ground. He was leaking. A dark red puddle was widening beneath him. Grundel gave one last look up at the cabin before turning toward the frozen lake. He had to get back to that hole in the ice. If he didn't, he might end up hanging on a wall above somebody's fireplace – like some goddam moosehead. Whatever happened, Grundel wasn't going to let them get him.

Dead or alive, Grundel was getting away.

Marc Bozian was working on his book. He had tentatively entitled it *The Turtle Terror of Turtleback Lake.*

Marc simply could not resist alliteration.

Meanwhile, Stephen Borg over at *The Record* had put Marc in contact with an agent who thought Marc's story – done right – could turn out to be more than a book. The agent, a young guy in the city named Mike Strong, thought there was potential for a movie – or maybe even a TV series.

"Think *Twin Peaks* meets *Jaws*," he wrote to Marc in an email. "See if you can work something up along those lines."

Marc loved all the Hollywood talk. He was thirty pages into his first draft when the attack at The Andersen cabin occurred. He covered it – for *The Record*. Borg had made him an offer he couldn't refuse.

Frankly, Marc couldn't believe his luck. It was as if the gods were helping him. In terms of death, drama and gore, the final chapter of the snapper saga surpassed any before it. The great snapper claimed two more victims – their bodies trapped beneath the ice with no hope of recovery until spring. Once again – and this was good – alcohol played a key role in the victims' deaths. It added a moral dimension that Marc liked.

And this was the very best part. The presumed-to-be-dead monster got to die a second death – this time at the hands of JJ Clayton – himself a snapper-attack survivor – using August Andersen's grandfather's ax! You couldn't make this stuff up!

For all the mayhem and misfortune that the turtle had caused the town of Turtleback Lake, it had all been a gift to Marc. Without the snapper, he might still be covering grand openings and town council meetings.

Of course, it was somewhat unsettling that neither the turtle nor the ax had been recovered. Still, the creature's blood spoor had stretched almost a mile. In fact, it was actually frozen into the ice: a red path that started near the Andersen cabin on the western shore and ended at the fishing hole where Ted Tanner and Bobby Savarese had vanished. No creature could lose that much blood and survive. Nobody was arguing that – at least not publicly.

"How much blood do you think a creature like that could have in its veins?" Deena asked August one night as they lay in bed.

"I don't know," he answered. "It's hard even trying to guess how much blood it lost that night. Unless…"

"Unless what?" asked Deena.

"Unless all the ice with blood in it was collected and thawed. Then the blood could be separated out and measured."

"You're not actually thinking of doing that, are you?" said Deena.

"No," said August. "It was just an idea."

And soon it was too late even for that.

Chief Rudolph had banned ice fishing for the remainder of the winter, but he had said nothing about ice-skating. Soon, sharp steel blades, crisscrossing over the frozen blood, scratched most of it away. Nobody would ever collect or measure Grundel's blood.

Chapter 26

Turtleback Lake January 2007

THE VIEW OF THE LAKE from the Claytons' living room was breathtaking. But JJ and Mary weren't looking at it. They were curled up on the couch with their eyes glued to the face of a grandfather clock that was ticking off the last minute of the year.

Together they counted down the last ten seconds.

"Ten, nine, eight, seven, six, five, four, three, two, one!"

When the clock struck twelve, fireworks exploded in the dark sky above the frozen lake. Streaming colors rained down, illuminating the revelers who had gathered on the ice below. Their cheers and the booming fireworks echoed off the mountainsides.

JJ snuggled closer to Mary. Their eyes closed as their lips met.

Suddenly, JJ let out a low moan. Mary opened her eyes and smiled.

"That felt *that* good?" she said.

"Yes," said JJ. "It did. But that's not why I moaned. I just felt something – like somehow the snapper is truly and finally gone."

Mary eased JJ down onto his back. She untucked his shirt and lifted it up. The scabs across his stomach, so raw and ugly just a few weeks before, were now fading. Mary gently traced the streaks with her fingertips.

And then, in a soft chanting voice, she whispered into JJ's ear.

"Hey, ho, snapper guy, now it's time you said goodbye."

And it was true. The great snapper was finally gone from the waters of Turtleback Lake.

In the spring, after the lake had thawed, the town hired specialists to remove the graffiti from Turtleback Rock. Also in the spring, they found – and buried – bits and pieces of Tanner and Savarese that had floated to the surface.

By summer, even the local real estate market had rebounded. Judd Clayton, as always, got most of the new listings. He even handled the sale of the former Burt bungalow. August Andersen had asked Deena to come back with him to Ithaca. She had said, "Yes," in a heartbeat and gave the high school two weeks notice the next day.

The baby that came in the spring was a bit of a surprise, but a most pleasant and welcome one. They named it Isaac Owen Andersen. Its eyes were neither green like August's nor brown like Deena's. They were a Nordic blue.

The color secretly troubled Deena.

"Eye color can change over time," said August. "Who knows what color they'll eventually end up?"

When Deena and August came to spend that summer in August's cabin, they stopped by to see Judd at Clayton Realty.

"What a beautiful baby," said Judd, looking at the bundled infant cradled in Deena's arms.

The coo of a newborn caught the ear of Judd's new assistant. She popped out of the supply closet. She was a tall slender blonde in shimmering pink shorts.

"What beautiful eyes," she said, looking at little Isaac Owen. "They're as blue as yours, Judd."

Deena felt a brief pang of panic but then Judd quickly cut in.

"I don't know whether either of you have ever met my neighbor," said Judd. "Deena and August, this is Connie Konsulis. She started working here a few months ago."

Deena could tell from the way Judd and Connie looked at each other that they were more than just workmates. Something was going on between them. Deena was happy for Judd. He'd been lonely too long.

Judd hung a *"Be Back Soon"* sign on the door of his office and they all went down for a walk along the lakeshore. They took turns pushing the baby carriage. As they strolled along, JJ, Mary, and Ian Copeland joined them.

Off in the distance, out in the middle of the lake, two men were sitting in a rowboat. Nobody needed binoculars to know who they were. Bill Lupo and his old friend, Oscar Hall, had become fishing buddies. Oscar went with Bill every time he went out. As the party on shore looked on, Bill caught a fish. It was a pickerel. Oscar took it off the hook and tossed it back into the lake. If only they had kept and cleaned it, they would have discovered a shiny bullet lodged in its digestive tract.

Beyond the two old anglers was Turtleback Rock. It was once again the landmark it had always been: white, sun bleached – with rumors of whirlpools swirling around it. A couple of small snappers lazed on its surface, basking in the sun.

August's mind dived under the surface of the lake to the labyrinth he had discovered in the mountain beneath the rock. He thought maybe one day he might explore it again.

And if he does, and if he goes far enough, August will make an astounding discovery: The other end of the tunnel is more than a mile away, on the far side of a mountain, in another lake.

There have been no reported attacks by a giant snapper there... *yet.*

www.ingramcontent.com/pod-product-compliance
Lightning Source LLC
Chambersburg PA
CBHW050926120626
46552CB00001B/55